TulipTree review

SPRING/SUMMER 2025
issue #17

Wild Women

TULIPTREE
PUBLISHING, LLC

Copyright © 2025 TulipTree Publishing, LLC
Mansfield, Missouri
Publisher & Editor in Chief, Jennifer Top

ISBN: 978-1-962812-04-7

www.tuliptreepub.com

Contents

Rainbow Sprinkles

Allyson Petrek

My mother wasn't speaking to me on the day my husband died. I don't even remember what she was mad about.

That night, I called her, and she didn't answer. Then I called again and again. On my fourth attempt, she answered the phone with a, "Stop pestering me, it's late," before promptly ending the call.

Jack had insisted on driving to get ice cream for us. It was a warm, summer evening, one full of lightning bugs and cricket chirps and heavy air that clung to your skin, and since I was in my thirteenth week of pregnancy, the thick blanket of exhaustion and nausea smothering my entire personality had finally slipped off.

He was going to drive up the street to the local Whippy Dip, the little ice cream stand where all the families in town went, where they ordered soft serve to celebrate home runs and straight A's and birthdays, where teenagers went on first dates, sitting with knees grazing each other beneath the sticky, wooden picnic tables, and where Jack wanted to commemorate the successful end of our baby's first trimester. We had planned to tell our families about the pregnancy the next day, given that my mom would actually speak to me.

The ice cream thing was his idea, and he pitched it to me, giddy like a sugar-crazed, six-year-old boy begging his mama. "Let's go," he said, pulling at my hand. "Let's celebrate."

I laughed and shook him off. "Hell, no," I said. "I'm feeling better, but that doesn't mean I feel like putting on real pants or standing in a line."

But, his eyes danced, and he offered, "Well then, I'll go by myself. I'll grab it and come right back, and we can go back to watching our show."

"You *sure*?" I remember asking. Without a doubt, I asked that. It's important—that I asked if he was sure.

He said, "Of course. Yeah, I'll be back in a flash. They're about to close."

"Okay," I said, snuggling deeper into the couch cushions—wholly, completely, and blissfully ignorant.

"What do you want?" he asked.

I pressed my lips together, imagining the yellow lights shining against the old, wooden menu board painted in chipped, cursive lettering. "Hmmm," I said, rubbing my chin, "I want vanilla, in a cup. With rainbow sprinkles."

"You want rainbow sprinkles," he repeated, deadpan. Then, his eyebrows popped up. "What are you, five?"

A snort-laugh erupted from the back of my throat. What a rich accusation from the thirty-five-year-old man who begged for soft serve. "What? I'm *pregnant*. Pregnant people crave weird things, okay?" I loved that newfound excuse, although it was only an excuse. I had always enjoyed sprinkles on my ice cream; they added texture. Frankly, I was surprised he didn't already know that about me. "Plus," I added, "I know if I asked for the whole sundae—with chocolate sauce and whipped cream and a cherry on top—they'd charge, like, an extra dollar twenty-five, and diapers are expensive, you know?"

Now it was his turn to laugh. His laugh was low and loud and vibrated in my bones like thunder on a summer night. "You're worth it," he said. Then he scooped a kiss off the top of my head and added, "Be right back."

I didn't get up to hug him or walk him to the door. I didn't tell him I loved him or that he was my best friend or my whole life.

I should have.

Because he wasn't *right back*. He didn't come back at all.

And then, later, when I called my mom to tell her he died on his way home with my goddamn rainbow sprinkles, she wouldn't answer the phone.

Could I have texted her? Sure. Could I have called her husband and told him what happened so she would call back? Of course.

But, I didn't want to have to convince my own mother to talk to me so that I could ask her to go with me to the hospital where my husband's dead body was.

So, I called my mother-in-law, Mary, instead, who I probably always was going to call next, after getting off the phone with my mother, but since my mother wasn't speaking to me, there was no buffer between finding out my husband had died on his way home from getting ice cream and telling a woman her son had died.

Which, by the way, she wasn't any woman. Mary may have well been the mother of God, and Jack may have well been Jesus Christ himself because they were truly that *good* and pure of a family.

Mary overwhelmed the shit out of me with her upright posture and coordinated outfits that looked like they came straight off the mannequins from the old lady section of the department store. The *classy* old lady section.

Her hair was always perfect, she had regularly scheduled facials and practically every other spa service I knew of, and I figured she probably even got waxed *down there*, although I had no idea at what point old ladies' pubic hair stopped growing. She was a soft-spoken, church-going, buttoned-up woman who was as vanilla as that milky-white soft serve I never got. In her family history, there was no divorce, save for that one cousin who "accidentally" married an alcoholic (*bless her heart*), no weird syndromes, birth defects, or chronic illnesses, and certainly no early, tragic deaths.

Until Jack, of course. He died in a car accident less than two miles away from home, on dry pavement in the dead of summer, at thirty-five, before he ever even got to feel his baby kicking in the womb.

Which I'd say counts as early and tragic.

By this point, when I called Mary, it was close to midnight, and I hadn't wrapped my mind around the ugly truth or uttered the words out loud—that Jack was dead—and when she answered the phone, not with a bleary "hello" from someone who had been pulled from sleep, but rather a breathy, "Is everything okay?" my answer caught in my throat.

No.

I couldn't say it out loud. I couldn't say that *No, it's not okay. Nothing will ever be okay again. Jack is dead*, because it was like she already knew.

I imagined her waking up in her beautiful satin pajamas, looking at her phone, and realizing her daughter-in-law was calling at 11:55 pm with the immediate understanding that things were not okay.

At that moment, my breath knotted in my chest, I considered the simple act of hanging up. *Butt dial*, she'd think in the morning when the memory became clear. *Silly girl*, she'd tell herself when she thought about me accidentally calling her at midnight on a Saturday.

"Hello?" she said, as if she was realizing she didn't, in fact, answer the phone with the word.

Hang up, I told myself. *Now.*

"Everything okay?" she repeated. Her voice was clearer, louder. I could tell she was sitting upright now, her legs swung over the side of the bed, perfectly painted toenails gripping the plush bedroom carpet.

A blinding heat wrapped itself around my vocal cords, and all I could do was shake my head. Of course, she couldn't hear it, but she must have somehow heard me—maybe my breath, maybe my tears (were there tears?)—because she didn't hang up.

And, finally, when I was able to choke out in a whisper, "There's been an accident," a low, guttural scream exploded from my phone, so loud that I dropped it and dug my fingernails into my scalp, trying to block out the sound of the scream. It didn't sound like it came from a human, and it certainly didn't sound like it came from my vanilla mother-in-law with her crucifix necklace and white teeth and freshly trimmed bob.

I don't remember much about the next few weeks. It was like I was living outside of my own body, watching things happen to me, completely unsure of the truth of my own memories.

For instance, I *thought* I remembered what the inside of the car looked like after the accident, although I never saw it.

That evening, after too much time had passed, after I had already made up excuses in my head for Jack taking forever getting the ice cream (*Oh, there must have been a line; someone's baseball game went into extra innings . . . Oh, someone must have called in sick; the shop must be short-staffed . . .*) and after I had already called him a half-dozen times, panic bubbling up my throat much like magma pressurizing the top of a volcano, I got in my car and began to drive in the direction of the Whippy Dip, down the winding, high-speed road we lived on.

I saw the flashing lights on the hill, a jumbled mess of electric blue and red, and I knew. Even before I saw his car, mangled in the ditch, I knew.

I never saw the inside of his car; it was towed away. But, for the next few weeks, I kept picturing rainbow sprinkles stuck to the ceiling. It was a crystal clear, vivid memory, alive in my mind, but I had no idea if I dreamt it or imagined it or if I, in fact, had seen it and had forgotten about seeing it, and the presence of these sprinkles itching my brain every time I closed my eyes was making me feel like I had gone insane.

However, there was one memory I knew actually happened. It happened on the day of the funeral. I wore an old black dress, one I had previously worn to Jack's cousin's wedding. (Certainly, not the cousin whose marriage ended in the D-word.) It wasn't a maternity dress, because my bump was still nonexistent. I was only fourteen weeks pregnant with my first child, and morning sickness and grief had eaten away at my flesh.

My mother had spent the day by my side. After she found out about Jack, she was playing her dutiful part as my caretaker, pure guilt fueling her intentions, never uttering a word of the fight we had been in.

We were sitting after the service, after the burial, after lunch, at a round table in a deserted basement of a church—the same one Jack grew up attending and the same one my mother bristled at when Jack and I decided to get married in front of its traditional, ornate altar— my mother on one side of me and Mary on the other, each of their husbands next to them. We were all exhausted from a long day with hundreds of people offering us their condolences, hugs, handshakes, and tears. Jack was both young and good, which was a recipe for a standing-room-only funeral.

I knew it was time; I needed to tell them.

So, in the quiet of the afternoon, in the dark of the basement, I said, "Everyone should know, I'm pregnant."

There were a few long seconds when no one said a word. They all just looked at me, not even attempting to mask their horror. Cheers, tears, and hugs would have been expected in a normal situation. But, this, of course, was not normal.

I filled the empty space with what I intended to be a quick explanation, but words kept spurting out like water from a busted pipe. "We were going to tell you. The day after Jack died. But things were a mess, and I thought I might lose it. You know, with all the stress. But, somehow, the baby's still sticking in there. I think."

They blinked at me.

Finally, after a moment where I didn't yell, "*Just kidding! Ha, you should have seen your faces*," my mother leaned over and kissed my temple, and both Jack's dad and my mother's husband seemed to grunt and nod and offer half-smiles.

Then, Mary reached out and touched my stomach—which felt terrifyingly invasive, like she was cupping her hand against the pudge that I didn't have and the extra helping of funeral potatoes that I didn't eat—and she said, low enough that my mother leaned in to hear her as well, her eyes red-rimmed and glassy, "Take care of our baby. You *must* take care of our baby. We *need* this baby."

I don't know if it was the fact that I was so shocked by this gesture, the intrusion of anyone's hand on my gut, uninvited, for the first time ever, or the fact that she called it "our baby," but I will always remember the look in her eyes when she said it.

Her eyes were frantic, wild. Unhinged.

That look. That was raw truth, something that will be burned into my memory forever.

Several months later, once the heat of the summer had long faded, Mary asked if she could throw me a baby shower. She had, at least seemingly, regained her composure. I figured she had caught up with her manicures, highlights, dry cleaning, and dusting, and that she was back to making her pie crusts for the church bake sale from scratch.

After a few weeks of blurred, spotty vision, I, too, attempted to resume normalcy, to go back to work, to bury myself in the mundane. I read up on how grief can impact a child in utero, from mental health issues later in life to heart problems to premature birth and all the risks that follow, so I largely pretended as though Jack was still around—perhaps on a vacation or work trip. I couldn't let myself feel;

I couldn't let myself break. After all, in the words of Mary: We *needed* this baby.

If there was one word I could have chosen to describe how those first months went as a pregnant widow, it would have been *unprepared*.

I used to have this dream, back in college and even in the first few years out of college, where I would step into a classroom, and the professor would announce that there was an exam that day, and I reeled, blindsided. I hadn't studied, didn't know the material, and didn't know there was an exam. Pure, evil panic would slip in, and I would wake up a sweaty, breathless mess. I'd blink, reminding myself it was a dream and rationalizing how it would never happen to me.

That feeling—of being wholly and completely *unprepared*—was a constant in the first few months after Jack passed. I kept waiting to wake up so that I could realize it could never happen to me. I *needed* to wake up so that Jack could show me how to pay the water bill and where to buy gas to fill the leaf blower, if it even took gas, and what to do when the upstairs toilet's flusher would get stuck and the thousand other things I realized I needed him for, including researching what kinds of things we needed to take a baby home in a few months. He always took care of me—of *us*. It was what I loved about him most of all.

So, I said yes to Mary, but promptly called my old college roommate, who already had three children, and asked her to help me register for the shower. When we did so, I handed her the beeper thingy and let her create my registry for me.

When my mother received the invitation for the shower, she invited herself over, as she tended to do, stuck her bottom lip out in a horrifying display of petulance, and said, "Well, *I* am your mother, the grandmother-to-be. I won't be going to this shower because *I* will be throwing you a baby shower, as well."

"You're only doing this because Mary's doing it," I pointed out. "You had no interest in throwing a baby shower until you felt left out."

"I didn't think baby showers were still a thing."

"You didn't think baby showers were still a *thing*?" I parroted. "Mom, that's ridiculous."

"Or, I didn't think you'd want one. You know, with everything that's happened."

"Just admit that you felt left out. I'm sure if you called her, she'd be thrilled to help you plan it. She's like that."

"Oh, for Christ's sake. I don't want to *help her plan it*. I want to throw my only daughter a baby shower."

"You're a little late," I said. Throughout my entire life, she was a little late—to everything, for everything. "Plus, who are you going to invite, Mom?" I asked. "I invited all my friends to Mary's shower, and I don't want to make them go to two showers. And I think my work is doing something, too. Forget about it."

"Well, we have family, too," she said, chin high in the air.

I sighed from the back of my throat, considering which "family" she was referring to. Probably her friends, conspiracy theorist Jennifer and crazy Helen, and Jojo, our ancient ex-neighbor, all of whom were in no way related to us, and maybe her cousins Sue and Nancy, who I *think* were related to us, although I hadn't seen them in years, and probably Nancy's weird daughter (what cousin does that make her with me?) with the nipple piercing and lip tattoo.

When Mary's shower came around, I wore a floral maternity dress, my stomach bulging, hair crimped in soft waves, and I smiled politely at all the people who came: Jack's countless aunts and cousins and Mary's friends and my friends. I made small talk and nodded at their kind compliments. I nibbled on tea sandwiches and sugar cookies with delicate frosting crafted into roses and pearls and opened gifts wrapped in thick, shiny paper while seated in a plush rocking chair, sunshine streaming in through large windows. It was lovely and sweet and everything I could have asked for in a baby shower.

Except, of course, that not a single one of those women so much as breathed Jack's name. His presence, or non-presence, was the big, fat elephant taking a shit in the middle of the room, and no one even glanced toward it.

It was like he never existed. And, I missed him.

Throughout the entire shower, I bit my lip the whole time, swallowing at regular intervals, trying to make the lump in my throat go away, steeling myself against the tears that crowded my vision, telling myself that I could not ruin my makeup.

As people were packing up to leave, I excused myself to the bathroom, where I hyperventilated with my head hanging over the toilet bowl, catastrophizing about the fact that there would be no surprise "drop-in" where my husband would stop by to kiss me on the cheek and tell me how beautiful I looked. He wouldn't thank all the guests or help me load the gifts into the car. And he wouldn't proceed to go home to build a crib and bassinet and changing table with his dad muscles clenched around a tiny non-screwdriver screwdriver (what were those even called?) and the rational ability to read an instruction manual written only in pictograms.

I couldn't ignore the truth, even if all the other people at the party could. Jack wasn't there and never would be.

A few weeks later, I went to my some-level-removed cousin Nancy's house for the other shower, where we sat outside on plastic lawn chairs on an early winter afternoon around a fire, blankets draped across laps, and everyone but me got drunk as they sipped on sweet, pink wine in plastic cups, and they asked me strange, intrusive questions like what my belly button looked like these days and if I ever peed my pants—even a little. They asked me how many cup sizes my breasts had grown because *Goddamn, they look good* and about the color and size of my areolas and what I planned to do with the placenta.

I squirmed as they asked, and when they got a bit drunker, they got a bit louder and I got a bit quieter, sitting back and listening to their conversations like a scientist observing the strange female friendships of *Homo sapiens* in the wild.

It was not perfect. It was not sweet. But, somehow, it didn't fill me with the same dread and fear and sadness that Mary's shower did.

My mother sat next to me, her sheer scarf ruffling in the breeze, hair a teased-out mess of curls, fierce gray hairs sticking out randomly, her hand protectively wrapped around my wrist.

At one point, after all the women shared their traumatic birth stories and their friends' traumatic birth stories and gave all kinds of unsolicited advice I hoped to forget immediately, Nancy looked straight at me, the smile dropping off her lips, and said, "You know, you're going to be okay. You can do this without him."

The whole circle of women seemed to shift in their seats, abandoning their laughter and smiles, and sobered instantly.

My stomach clenched at the verbal reminder that I was not okay and Jack was not here. I bit my lip.

"It sucks for everyone," she added. "Birth, postpartum. It sucks. But you'll be okay. Your baby will be okay."

The women all nodded in agreement, although no one said anything. They sat silently, throwing their glances between Nancy and me.

"I know," I managed.

"Jack is proud of you, you know," added my mother. She rubbed her hand against my shoulder. "He loves you."

A tear dropped out of my eye, unexpectedly. I squeezed my eyes shut, but more tears came, faster and louder, and a wrinkled tissue magically appeared, pressed into my hand by one of these strange ladies.

There was a comfort in it—in crying, in letting go of the tears I held in. I felt hands on my shoulders and whispers in my ear saying, "It's okay."

Crying at that moment, in front of everyone, felt like releasing a breath I didn't know I was holding. The tears came tumbling out, uncontrolled. I had no strength left to stop them.

After a few long, quiet minutes of everyone watching me cry, I released a shaky sigh, dried my face, and said, my voice barely above a whisper, "Thanks, everyone."

"You can do it. And you will," said Nancy, repeating her earlier sentiment, head bobbing, eyes fixed on mine.

I nodded and continued to dab at my face with the wet tissue. "Sorry, everyone. I try not to cry," I explained, "but I can't help it sometimes. I know it's bad for the baby."

Suddenly, everyone had something to say, as if I had just confessed to something terribly taboo, like using plastic straws or flushing tampons or earmarking the pages of library books, and they did so by shouting over each other.

"Horseshit!"

"Who told you that?"

"Don't be ridiculous."

I put my hands up in tentative surrender, feeling heat creep up my neck, and said, "*Jesus*, everyone. I Googled it. And learned that excessive stress on the mother can really damage the unborn baby."

Again, the shouting.

"Don't Google it, then!"

"If that were the case, how has the human race survived?"

"We should all be dead."

"Damaged, she said *damaged*."

Sue spoke up this time, waving them off with an *I-got-you-guys* nod, and then said, "Honey, do you know what's bad for the baby? Barbiturates and narcotics and marijuana and alcohol and tobacco."

"*Allegedly*," added Jennifer with a finger raised to the sky.

"Tobacco never hurt *you*. At least, not too much," said Nancy in a stage whisper, elbowing her daughter, who received her words with a dramatic eye roll.

"That's not the way I raised you to think," interjected my mother. "We don't bury our feelings because Google told us to."

I looked down at the tissue in my hand, which was disintegrating between my fingers. I had no idea how to wrap up a party I wasn't hosting, but I suddenly wanted to go home. The temperature was too high in the oven and I was overcooked.

My mother seemed to sense it, because she softened her face, wrapped her cold fingers around mine, and squeezed. "It's okay to live in your grief," she said, dropping her voice low, "to *acknowledge* your feelings."

"Okay. You know how I feel?" I said, my voice trembling. "*Scared*. Scared out of my mind."

"You're allowed to feel scared," my mother said, nodding.

"And *sad*. I'm so sad. I miss Jack with every breath in my body. And I feel guilty that I'm sad and I'm missing him, that I'm not giving my baby everything I should."

"It's okay to feel sad," she said. "Or angry or lonely. There's no right way to feel. And none of it changes the fact that you're going to be a great mother."

"Which you already are," added Nancy. The sound of her voice, breaking into what seemed like a private conversation with my mother, surprised me. I looked at her.

And then, I looked around. The other women were all looking on, continuing to nod gently.

I wasn't sure if this was the tribe—the village—that I wanted, but they were here, wrapping their support around me. And, since there was no right way to feel, I sat with the wind blowing through my hair and a single thought whispering through my brain: I felt a little bit like myself for the first time since Jack died.

If I had felt unprepared in the weeks and months following Jack's death, I don't know the word to properly describe how I felt in the days and weeks leading up to the baby's birth. *Unprepared* didn't begin to cover it.

My mother, in her typical erratic, unpredictable fashion, announced to me when I was thirty-six weeks pregnant that she would be going to some antique convention eight hours away with Sue that next weekend.

"Mom, I'll be thirty-seven weeks. You can't leave me," I said, my voice squeaking. "What if I go into labor?"

"Oh, for Christ's sake," she said, "this is your first baby. You probably won't go until well over forty weeks, like I did with you. It'll be a whole 'nother month before you have this baby. Plus, I'm still planning on moving in with you after I get back. I'll be there when you go into labor, and I'll live with you for the first month after she arrives. It's not like you're not going to *miss* me."

I rolled my eyes at her for many reasons. Firstly, that she thought going on a vacation at this point in my pregnancy was a good idea. Secondly, that she insisted on the fact that the baby was a "she," for absolutely no reason other than my mother "just knew," and thirdly, that she planned to live with me for *more* than a month. A month was an unbearable amount of time to deal with her ear-piercing laugh, passive-aggressive remarks, and refusal to wear real deodorant.

When I went to my next OB appointment, my mother had already left, and my blood pressure was through the roof after a sudden incline the doctor had been "keeping an eye on"—unsurprising when you think of the conditions of the pregnancy—and there was protein in my urine and my toes were bloated like little sausages, so the doctor told me I would be heading to the hospital. I would be induced that afternoon.

I called my mom as I drove myself to the hospital. She didn't answer, so I called Mary, remembering her hand on my stomach, pleading with me that *we need this baby*, and I told her I needed her. It actually had always been the plan: that Mary and my mother would be there to welcome their grandbaby into the world. But, it turned out that Mary would be there and my mother would be browsing old china patterns.

My mother eventually did call back, hours later, once the medicines had started to *ripen* my cervix (their word, not mine), and I told her I was in the hospital, waiting to *ripen*, and that she should start driving here *right-the-fuck-now*.

She, calmly and assertively, with complete confidence in her non-medical medical knowledge, told me that inductions take "forever"—most likely, multiple days—and she'd be there in the morning with plenty of time to spare before I'd need her.

Of course, the baby decided not to listen to its grandmother's non-medical medical knowledge.

Things moved slowly for a long time, throughout the evening and several hours into the early hours of the morning, and then labor came hard and fast, like my body recognized what was about to happen and decided it was ready to evacuate my womb immediately. Suddenly, like a green banana that speckles brown overnight, my water broke and I puked all over the bed, started violently shaking, and begged for the nurse to fetch the anesthesiologist.

Mary was the perfect birthing coach and partner—almost like she had prepared for the event by reading books and listening to seminars on how to be the perfect support system. (Which, I recognized, she probably did.) She was steady, kind, and encouraging. She let me mangle her fingers in my sweaty grip, shout curse words in her ear, and in some superhuman exercise, didn't eat or sleep that night. And she never complained, not once.

In brutal honesty, she was a better birthing coach than Jack would have been, seeing as though he would have eaten at least two meals in front of me and definitely would have caught a not-so-quick nap on the couch and probably a not-so-quick shit on the toilet, and she sure as hell was better than my mother would have been, seeing as though my mother would have pulled gummies laced with god-knows-what from her purse and attempted to trick me into eating them.

That being said, when the doctor announced it was time to start pushing, tears tore down my cheeks and I begged him, "Can we wait?

Let's wait. My mom isn't here and my husband is dead and this is too fast, faster than it's supposed to happen. This is not normal."

But, the doctor chuckled and shook his head, seemingly mocking me in his mind, and then explained, "Every labor is different. It's hard to say anything is normal."

I chewed on the words for a moment, letting them replay in my head. *It's hard to say anything is normal.* Then, giant, blindingly bright lights came down from the ceiling, and he suited up, pulling on a gown and gloves as if he were about to hop in his Batmobile and save Gotham, and he announced with a grin I wanted to slap off his face, "Let's rock and roll."

Everyone in the room—and there suddenly was an excess of people in the room—could see from the monitor attached to my stomach that another contraction was about to begin, and Mary leaned over and whispered, breath hot in my ear, "I'm sorry he's not here."

I opened my mouth, ready for my turn to apologize, *I'm sorry that I'm the one who asked for rainbow sprinkles*, but the next contraction seized control, wrapping intense pressure around my body, and the doctor interrupted any thought I had, shouting, "Okay, now! Push!"

To which, I wanted to shout back that I didn't know *how* to push out a baby, but my body actually did seem to know. And the nurse held my one knee, counting loudly, and Mary held my other. And I forgot all about how I didn't want my well-groomed mother-in-law to stare at my non-waxed pubic region because all I cared about in the entire world was getting the baby out *right-the-fuck-now*.

And we repeated that scene with several more contractions. Was it minutes? Hours? I had no idea, but when the baby arrived, there was a blinding moment of relief as I heard a high-pitched wail and I couldn't see anything, because tears had masked my sight.

They put her on my chest, and I think Mary must have cut the cord, but I was overwhelmed with this distinctive feeling of surprise:

that the baby was, in fact, a human baby and not some alien creature as I had imagined. She blinked and squirmed against my bare chest, screaming and crying and gasping for breath, all fingers and toes and cottage cheese skin folds.

When she calmed down, Mary and I looked at each other in wild-eyed wonder. And, the birth was over as quickly as it had begun.

An hour or so later, they wheeled me and my baby into a private recovery room, and my new nurse pointed out the restroom and announced to me that, whenever I needed to urinate, I needed to call for assistance getting to the toilet, and I should do the deed in the plastic bucket that was currently attached to the toilet seat. She warned me that I needed to pee in the next few hours, and not to be alarmed: There would be a *lot* of blood.

"Okay, no problem," I said, nodding, but still focused on holding the baby, now asleep, against my chest.

But it was a problem. Christ, was it a problem.

Time slipped by. The baby slept and I basked in her warmness, stilling myself to feel her tiny, perfect breath, shallow against my skin.

Eventually, I realized I would need to set her down to try my assigned task of peeing in the bucket, so I called for assistance and a nurse came to walk me to the toilet.

As I stood up, the world felt new, slightly wobbly. I felt empty and raw. Sore, stiff. Not just the entire bottom half of my body—the whole thing, every single muscle—was singing in pain.

Why had no one told me? I had heard so many birth stories and seen so many snippets of childbirth portrayed in books and on screen, but why had no one told me quite what it felt like *after* the baby came out? How had I attended birth classes and read books and listened to podcasts, and I had no idea that the real pain began *after* I had been cleaned and stitched and wheeled down the hall? The pain from labor only lasted a handful of hours; my body would be recovering from it forever.

I wanted to look in the mirror, to hold the coarse hospital gown up and see my babyless stomach for the first time, but the nurse hung outside the door, so I sat down to pee, legs quivering, and tried to do something I had been doing for over thirty years.

But, nothing happened; I couldn't do it. And I needed to go.

The nurse said, "No worries. We'll try again in a bit," and she walked me back to the bed and left.

So, I waited and then tried again.

And again.

Before the nurse left the third time, I asked what would happen if I couldn't pee, and she shrugged and said they'd "cath" me. *Cath* me. She said it with utter nonchalance, as if doling out a single Tylenol and not a needle down *there*.

That's when I started to panic. I'm not sure why; I had completely welcomed the idea of getting a giant needle up my spine earlier, but all rational thought had evaporated from my brain.

Mary, who was still in the room, said, "Ah, don't worry, dear. You heard the nurse. Catheters are very common in hospitals."

I stared at her, hard, and said, in complete seriousness, "What if I never pee again?"

She chuckled and said, "Oh, stop stressing. If you stress about it, it'll make it harder to go."

You know what you really don't want to hear when you're stressed about something? *Stop stressing*. I could have killed her right then if I didn't think killing a woman who would one day be canonized a saint would send me straight to hell.

Panic pressed down on me, and my heart was beating in my teeth. At that moment, a tiny, strange doll slept soundlessly in the plastic-sided bassinet in the corner of the room, my husband was dead, my mother was nowhere to be found, I hadn't slept in over twenty-four hours, I hadn't eaten since yesterday, and I was sinking into the obvious and rational assumption that I would never urinate again.

"She looks *exactly* like him," Mary then said, staring at the baby. "Doesn't she?"

My mouth fell open. Did she not understand the gravity of the situation? And, for the record, the baby looked like a wrinkly old man. A beautiful and precious wrinkly old man, but nevertheless one that certainly did not look like Jack.

I walked myself to the bathroom this time, slammed it shut, and turned on the sink. Then, I sat on the toilet and waited. And waited. I tried putting my fingers in the running water. I tried squirting myself with warm water with the squirt bottle they left for me. I tried taking deep breaths and humming and praying and wiggling my toes.

Then, I did the most obvious thing I could think of: I unlocked my phone and searched the all-knowing internet. *How to pee after delivering a baby*.

The first result I clicked? A post that told me to stop stressing.

Then I scanned through many, many posts on various forums that explained how catheters were no big deal and how common of an issue this was for a variety of reasons.

I saw a post suggesting sniffing peppermint oil, which sounded like a pleasant, noninvasive option, but I had no idea where the hell I'd find such a luxury in this institution filled with fluorescent lights and long, quiet hallways.

Eventually, I found a post on a forum that read, "*Try this: Bring a water cup with a straw into the bathroom. Sit on the toilet and blow bubbles into the cup with the straw. Voila! This should relax your pelvic floor so you can go.*"

I squinted at my phone screen. What kind of sorcery was that? Surely, blowing bubbles with my straw wouldn't magically make me pee. Plus, unlike what Jack had suggested, I wasn't five years old, and I certainly hadn't blown bubbles in my cup since that age.

But, my other options were limited to (A) my bladder exploding, which I figured was a likely impending situation, or (B) getting a needle shoved up my seemingly broken pee hole, so I pulled up my giant mesh underwear that was lined with a sanitary pad bigger than my baby, hobbled back into the room where the giant plastic cup of water sat on my bedside table, and picked it up.

As I turned to head back to the bathroom, I looked at Mary, who was hunched over the bassinet, taking a picture of the sleeping baby. She didn't even look at me, but instead mumbled, "Spitting image of Jack, I'm telling you. Spitting image."

I pretended I hadn't heard her and went directly back to the toilet. I sat down, brought my straw to my lips, and blew. As the bubbles started percolating in the cup, I felt it: warm relief. Urine sputtered into the plastic bucket.

When I had filled the bucket to the best of my abilities, I set the water cup down and leaned over, put my elbows on my knees, buried my eyes in my palms, and sobbed big, heaving breaths.

I knew it was the first of innumerable times I would have to figure this parenthood shit out on my own. The loneliness was instantly suffocating.

My mother arrived later that afternoon like a hurricane, blowing in with rushed apologies and a chaotic energy that edged on hysteria. She took my face in her hands and told me how beautiful I was and how proud she was, and shortly after her stormy arrival, Mary excused herself to go home and get some rest.

As soon as Mary stepped out, my mother looked at me, fire blazing behind her eyes, and said, "*She* may have gotten to be here for the birth of the baby, but *I* will be here for the birth of the mother," and she squeezed my hand and refilled my water, filling it to the top with those little ice nuggets I loved so much.

When the three of us—my mother, me, and the baby that I obviously was expected to name Jacqueline—went back to my house, she was, in fact, ready to catch me as I entered, slippery and screaming, into motherhood. She took care of me and I took care of Jacqueline, and when I couldn't take care of Jacqueline, because it was all too much, which it often was, she brought her, tenderly, into her arms and walked out of the room.

Once again, I felt utterly unprepared. Except, this time, I wondered if I would ever shake the feeling for the rest of Jacqueline's life.

Those first few days were a sleepless haze of unfamiliar odors, emotions, and bodily fluids, which made me realize why no one warned me of the early postpartum days. It was because no one could remember them, or, moreover, no one *wanted* to. This chapter of life could not be glamorized enough to be included on the movie or television screen. It could not be tamed enough to be written about in books or spoken about in podcasts. This chapter of life was reserved for blurry memories, living in the back of women's minds—an homage meant to build empathy and perspective.

In one of my fits of hormonal, sleep-deprived, overwhelmed, doom-and-gloom cry sessions, I was sobbing on the couch, so hard that I couldn't breathe, almost as if I was finally letting out all the tears I had held back when Jack first died, and my mother grabbed my face and told me, "Stop this. You were born to do hard things," and then wrapped her arms around me until I found my breath.

Mary stopped over daily, with homemade casseroles and bags of groceries, eager to hold a sleepy Jacqueline. She came with hands full of good intentions and kindness, but each time she came, she was put together in a way that made a glimmer of shame cast a heavy shadow across any progress I made. She sat on the couch in her slacks and sweaters, pearl earrings, and a full face of makeup while I pulled on an old robe reeking of spilled, bitter coffee and sour breast milk to cover up my chapped nipples, adult diaper, and otherwise naked body.

"Go, take a nap," she'd say, waving me off. "Or, a shower," she'd add with a wink.

But, I didn't want to. I wanted to keep Jacqueline within catching distance in case someone dropped her.

At night, I stared at her, watching for her breath. When I couldn't see her breathing, I placed my finger by her little nose, breath suspended in my own chest, waiting to feel air. She was so tiny and fragile and dependent that it seemed like death would come rushing back to our life at any moment.

The days and nights were long and repetitive, but we endured. My mother never complained, not once. She prepared meals and washed dishes and sheets and refilled my giant bottles of water that were strewn around the house. I even caught her, several times, re-organizing drawers, which felt intrusive and annoying, but I didn't have the energy to object.

After the first week, my stomach stopped cramping to the point of toe-curling pain and the swelling in my fingers dissipated enough that I could get my wedding ring back on. After two weeks, I stopped needing to take my water cup in the bathroom to blow bubbles and I could generally sit on the toilet without feeling like an organ was going to tumble out with a large splash. After three weeks, which felt like three years, my nipples stopped screaming in pain when Jacqueline would latch to breastfeed, I stopped needing to sit on ice packs, and my random crying outbursts managed to reduce to roughly once a day. By the time she was one month old, I had almost stopped bleeding, had learned to sleep on a towel to manage the night sweats, and found a mindless television show to keep me company during the middle-of-the-night feeds. And, one morning when Jacqueline was napping in her bassinet, my mother told me it was time for her to move back home.

"What?" I said, panic, my loyal friend, knocking at my chest. I stared at her suitcase, all packed up and ready to go, next to the front door. "Where are you going?"

"Home," she said with a dismissive frown. "It's time. I said I'd stay a month with you, and now you have things under control. I have to get back to my own life."

"But I need you *here*."

"Don't worry, I'll still visit. Plus, Mary's around the corner, and you like her better anyway."

"Jesus, Mom. I don't like her better."

"You invited *her* to the birth of *my* grandbaby, you know."

Sighing loudly, I twisted up my nose so she could see my irritation. Her version of the truth tended to deform with time, like a balloon leaking air.

I held the words in my mouth, the ones that said *I did invite you; you were the one who wasn't there,* because I could tell she was picking a fight. I knew she wanted to make me mad so—in her warped little mind—I wouldn't actually miss her.

Which, of course, I would miss her. I remembered how, just over a month ago, the thought of living with my mother for a month was absurd. Now, I had no idea how I was going to figure this out without her, and I felt as if I were one of those babies they dropped in a pool to see if they would figure out how to float. Except, I was swallowing mouthfuls of water, and I missed her already even though she was standing right next to me.

We stared at each other for a long moment, until she asked, "Do you want to go outside?"

"Isn't it pretty cold out there?" I glanced out the window.

She gave a deep shrug, burying her neck in her shoulders. "Isn't it all about perspective? It's been a cold winter. This first touch of spring will feel like a heat wave."

I sighed. "I'll get my jacket."

Then I slipped the baby monitor into my pocket, poured myself a fresh cup of coffee, and we stepped onto my back deck.

It was the first time I'd been out there since late last year, and there was dirt and green fuzz crusted on the patio furniture. I cocked my head, looking at the four chairs around a filthy glass table, and wondered if Jack would have brought the furniture down to the basement for the winter. Probably. I thought that was something he used to do, but I'd never know, would I?

My mother pulled a dirty chair out with a loud, metallic *creak*, brushed it off with her palm—as if that would do anything to the fuzz issue—and sat down. I followed suit.

We sat in the early March breeze, not talking for a long while. I hated that she was right, that this first, somewhat warm day after months of winter felt like dropping a Molly at a rave, so I didn't say anything about it. But, I took big, deep breaths, letting the warm air fill my lungs with color and life.

Eventually, she said, "You'll be okay, you know?"

"If everyone keeps saying that, does it make it true?"

She pressed her lips together and looked around at my backyard. It was not beautiful. Without leaves on the trees, you could see directly into the neighbors' backyard, where bunches of bright, yellow daffodils speckled their flowerbeds. Mine were empty. The grass had started to turn green, but the sun was filtered by a lazy, white overcast, so it was not yet that electric, vibrant green that was so welcomed after a long winter.

"Wouldn't it be nice to have a flowering tree back here?" asked my mother, as if she read my mind.

I shrugged. "Sure. Don't know how I'm ever going to have time or energy to plant a tree," I said, and then, after a moment, repeated the clarifier, "*ever*."

"One day, you'll look back at this time, and you won't even remember how hard it all was."

"I highly doubt that."

"I'll plant one," she announced, nodding to herself. "Yes, my parting gift to you. Today, before I leave. What kind of tree would you like?"

"What? I don't want a tree."

"Jacqueline should have a flowering tree in her backyard."

"Mom, she's a month old and I don't want you to spend the day planting a tree I will kill. I don't have time to care for it."

"Well, then, we will get you something wild, native. How about a redbud? It's the right time of year to plant one."

"I don't know what a redbud is," I said, shaking my head.

"Oh, sure you do. It's the bright, pinky-purple understory tree you see on the edges of woods all around here. It's pretty, you'll like it."

"Mom, you're making work for us. Can we chill today?"

"You *chill* today. I'll take care of it."

I frowned but didn't object. I had learned throughout my entire life that nothing I could say would stop her from driving to the nursery, buying the damn tree, and planting it in my backyard.

"There's something poetic I love about redbuds," she said, apparently taking my silence for acquiescence. "Do you know what it is?"

I fought back the urge to roll my eyes. "No, what?"

"They don't flower unless there's a cold enough winter."

She stood up, brushed the seat of her pants off, and disappeared into the house. I sat, legs propped up on the table, and sipped my coffee, letting it warm me from the inside.

A few minutes later, Jacqueline's cry erupted over the baby monitor and I went inside to get her.

Several hours later, after multiple rounds of changing Jacqueline, nursing her, and putting her down for short-lived naps, I decided to wrap her up in a soft blanket, put a tiny hat on her, and carry her back outside with me. The sun had melted away the milky overcast from earlier in the day and was now shining brilliantly, tucked high in the bluebird sky.

Jacqueline had been fussing—already tired from her long day of eating, pooping, and sleeping—but as soon as we stepped onto the back deck, she calmed, looking to the sky with hazy wonder, transfixed by the sound of gentle bird calls and the wind bristling in the leafless trees. I held her close to my chest, nervous about shading her bare face from the sun, and worried if she was warm enough or too warm. But, after a few moments of staring at the bright sky, her eyes snapped shut, and she was once again asleep in my arms, an image of contentment.

I sat back down on the dirty patio chair, holding Jacqueline to my chest, and wondered if babies could miss the warm spring sun if all they've ever known was cold.

I watched as my mother draped a large net over a tiny stick of a plant that was tied to a metal stake in the middle of the yard. *"That's the tree?"* I whisper-shouted from my spot on the deck. "I thought you meant you were getting a *tree*-tree."

She stood up and brushed her palms together. "This is a tree-tree," she called back. "It'll get to be, like, twenty feet tall. I couldn't carry anything bigger. Do you know how heavy those trees are with the giant rootballs?"

I rolled my eyes and sighed. She walked up the two steps to where I sat on the deck, collapsing in the chair next to me.

"You know, we could have bought a bigger tree and hired someone to plant it," I said, glancing down at Jacqueline. "Is she still asleep?"

She looked over at us and then back to the stick. "She's out. And, it'll grow."

"How long until that thing resembles a real tree?"

"I mean, a while." She sighed. "Have you ever heard the sleep, creep, leap idea?" I shook my head, so she explained, "When trees are first planted, they appear to sleep for the first year. But, they really aren't sleeping or dead or whatever. They're busy underground, establishing roots. In the second year, they *creep*, appearing to grow very slowly. Then, the third year, that's when they *leap*, growing very quickly."

I nodded and looked down at Jacqueline. She was warm against my chest. And then I looked back at the ridiculous, caged stick in the yard, and I figured it was okay if the stick and I took this time—this season, this year—to "sleep." To grow our roots, to let them spread in the soft dirt.

Creeping and leaping? That could come later.

Just then, the back door opened, and Mary appeared, offering a meek wave as she stepped out onto the deck. "Hi," she said brightly. She stepped over to where we sat, eyed my dirty patio furniture, and stood beside me, looking down at the sleeping Jacqueline. "I was at the store, and it was *so* nice today, it felt like a good day to eat some ice cream, so I bought you a carton. I put it in your freezer."

I gave her a closed-lip smile. It had turned into an actual warm spring afternoon, and not just in a Midwestern spring type of way, but I was willing to bet Mary never ate ice cream, so did she really know what a good day to eat ice cream felt like? Plus, with all that happened in the past year due to ice cream, I didn't think I'd ever eat it again. But, I said, "Thanks, Mary. You know, you don't have to bring something over to visit. You can just come over."

"Oh, I know," she said. "I wanted to."

I exhaled. These stubborn-ass women would do whatever the hell they wanted, and it didn't matter what I said. At this point, they'd never be tamed.

"So, what's going on?" she added. "How is everyone?"

"Good," I said, nodding. "My mom is leaving today, and she decided to plant a stick for me in my backyard as a parting gift."

"It's a redbud," my mother corrected.

"Oh, that's lovely," said Mary, looking at the stick. "Do you need any help?"

My mother eyed Mary up and down, obviously judging her monochromatic cream outfit and leather loafers, and then said, "I think it's taken care of."

I threw her an annoyed, *let's-be-nice* look as Mary pulled out the dirty chair on the other side of me, eyed it carefully, and sat down with only the tiniest edge of her butt cheeks touching the seat. "Do *you* need any help?" she asked me.

I shrugged. "No. I think I'm okay right now. But, my mother is throwing me off the deep end by leaving me, so check back tomorrow," I said, raising my eyebrows playfully.

She offered a tight, kind smile, and said, "Of course, I'll check on you, and—"

"Me too," interjected my mother.

Mary gave the same smile to my mother and then continued, "But, she's right. It's probably time."

"See? It's time," echoed my mother.

"I'm just saying, you and Jacqueline need to figure things out, together. You'll think you can't do something and then—suddenly—you'll do it. Just like how she's going to grow and reach milestones, you will too." She held out her hand with a grabbing motion, and I realized she was reaching for mine, awkwardly, so I adjusted the sleeping Jacqueline with one hand and held out the other. She squeezed it, hard, and said, "We're so proud of you."

I nodded and smiled, blinking away the sudden wetness that had crowded my vision, but my mom abruptly dismissed what could have been a tender moment when she interjected with, "Ice cream actually sounds good. Who else wants some?"

Mary's face wrinkled—only for a second—and then she shook her head, relaxed her face, and said, "No, thank you."

I scowled hard at my mother and said, "I'm okay."

She stood up and walked to the door and into the kitchen. I prepared myself for Mary to ask to hold Jacqueline, but she didn't.

When my mother reappeared a few minutes later, she carried out three coffee mugs by their handles, three spoons sticking up, and set them down on the grimy table. I could see Mary glance down and frown at the ice cream she did not ask for, only to pick it up and cautiously dig her spoon in.

I shifted Jacqueline, draping her sleeping body higher on my chest so that I could eat the ice cream one-handed. I, too, dug my spoon into the cup, but, when the spoon came into view, I was surprised to see both ice cream and sprinkles on it. My heart hopped.

"Where did these sprinkles come from, Mom?"

"Your pantry. I reorganized it last week."

I said, "Oh. Those are probably expired."

"Sprinkles expire?"

I shrugged and opened my mouth as if to say something I couldn't quite find the words for. There was no way she knew about me asking Jack for sprinkles on the night of the accident. I had never told anyone about the sprinkles.

"You've always liked sprinkles on your ice cream," she said, answering the question I hadn't yet asked.

I nodded and closed my mouth. Of course, my mother would know that. She was my mother.

I took a bite of the ice cream. It wasn't some earth-shattering moment, where ice cream gave me a flashback of *that* night. It was simply a bite of ice cream. Cold and sweet and creamy. With sprinkles. Like I had been eating my entire life.

I don't know if my mom or Mary connected ice cream with *that* night, but at the moment, it seemed silly that I did. It was just ice cream. And it had been almost a year, and I couldn't *not* eat ice cream forever. Right?

We sat together, silently eating, the sun warming our skin, the ice cream chilling our bones, and I considered how long I had waited for these damn sprinkles.

Ever since the accident, I had thought my life would be split into two categories: "before Jack's death" and "after Jack's death," and I wasn't sure I'd ever be okay living in the *after* chapter.

But, as we sat there, I realized that all was wrong. There was only "before Jacqueline" and "after Jacqueline," and Jacqueline and I could be better than okay in our *after*. We would creep and leap and grow together after this temporary sleep.

I wished Jack could be here, to hold her and kiss her—to breathe in her warmth and newness—but she was lucky, as was I, to have the two grandmothers here, sitting on either side of us. They were each wild, fierce, in their own way. I hoped Jacqueline would inherit that from them. Maybe she'd be a little vanilla, a little rainbow sprinkles.

Actually.

I hoped she'd get to be the whole damn sundae. She was worth it.

Cedar Woman

Alexis Bonavitacola, PhD

New Jersey was sweltering, and power grids gave out that July. No amount of talcum powder soaked up the sweat beads, and the thought of traveling to a place hotter than the East Coast was considered pretty much insanity.

I was in transition again. Six months into a self-flagellating separation from S.—the man who taught me about pieds-à-terre and power—I shattered at minor things, tears coming fast and without permission. Couples strolled through the streets of New York, lost in each other, oblivious to the taxis screeching, the steam rising from the grates, and the entire city pulsing around them. Sometimes, when I thought I could hold it together, I'd hear Etta James belting out the words to "our" song. "At last, my love has come along. My lonely days are over. And life is like a song." I'd crumble. Again. Each tear carried the weight of something stupid I supposedly said during that marriage, and I knew my lonely days were SO NOT OVER.

Panic attacks seized me in strange places. In between handfuls of popcorn at the movies, I'd suddenly feel and hear the thump, thump, thump of my heart growing louder and quicker. "Oh my God, I'm dying. Having a heart attack right here, all A-L-O-N-E," I wailed inside. The *alone* word carried much more weight than any other word in the dictionary that summer.

I turned into the poster child for New Age love cures. In July, amid the candle healing, astrology charting, tarot cards, feng shui, palm readings, and rosary bead clutching, I danced with the Devil and was one step away from becoming a cloistered nun. I made sure I covered all of my bases. I played Let's Make a Deal with God and fell asleep to Marianne Williamson's New Age phenomenon, *A Return to Love*. I let her hypnotic voice assure me that she knew precisely how crappy I was feeling, and all I needed to do was confront my deepest fear, love myself, love and forgive every human being who ever knew me, and everything would be perfect. I was looking for miracles, not logic. Yeah, I read all about this place I was in. The Holy Grail of growth, so much learning going on, the neutral zone, the place of transition, Blah, blah, blah. I needed something life-changing. Now!

Carry-on luggage in one hand, balanced by your laptop computer in the other, you stride through the refrigerated airport. Determined yet anxious, you burst through the exit doors and find yourself assaulted immediately by oven-like heat. Your first inclination is to run back inside the Phoenix airport, find a Continental ticket agent, and book the next flight back to New Jersey. But, no, that is not an option for you. As you stand glued to the pavement, your pores immediately begin to open, and the nape of your neck becomes moist, wet, and dripping with sweat. You realize that you will evaporate into the sidewalk if you do not move soon. Almost running, you fumble for your now heated cell and try to call your mother before your fingers burn. "Mom," you gasp, "I am in Phoenix, and it's hot here. This is the Indian Sweat Lodge." Not grasping the whole reality of the broiling temperature, she laughs and says, "Oh, honey, I'm sure it's hot, but it's that dry heat, and you shouldn't feel it as much." You cough up the words and scream, "HEAT IS HEAT. WHEN IT'S 116 DEGREES, IT IS STILL HOT—EVEN IF IT'S DRY HEAT. PUTTING YOUR HEAD IN AN OVEN IS DRY HEAT, TOO!"

Searching for the rental car, you finally spot your transport vehicle for this journey and let out a loud, Thank You, Jesus! to anyone within earshot. Turning the ignition, you neglect to heed the rules of

Automotive 101 and immediately spike the air conditioner to bone-chilling coldness. You pray it doesn't get any hotter than this. You know differently.

Was this hell, I wondered? Dante's Inferno? When I still hadn't convinced S. to go back with me, even with promises of being the future Stepford wife of his dreams, I resorted to eradicating any demons of individuality I owned. I figured that a few hours of sweating and chanting with my ancestral spirits and a few other like-minded-screwed-over-looking-for-love-in-all-the-wrong-places women would do me some good. As they say, misery loves company.

I met Tammy that weekend in Sedona at a women's retreat, a spiritual quest and a search for answers. We came from various geographic points—Texas, Florida, California, and New Jersey. Significant life transitions were the only passports we needed. From the minute Tammy entered the house, I immediately liked her Dallas, Texas, kick-ass spirit and knew that even if the weekend were a bust, Tammy would be a good time. "Hi, honey," she said. "Whatcha here for?" Tammy's drawl was warm, like sweet honey, and one of those sexy mama types oozing with that I've-been-around-the-block-a-few-times attitude in her voice. Tammy had perfect, in-place auburn hair pulled back in a ponytail. She reminded me of one of those pageant contestants, and it wasn't a stretch for me to think of her as a former Miss Texas. Everything about her was put together: coral manicured pedi and mani, makeup done to a T, dewy lipstick that matched her nails, tight black slacks, and a turquoise knitted top that showed off one of those to-die-for figures. At 48 years young, she looked spicy hot and reeked of confidence.

Leading up to the sweat lodge experience, Tammy let the other ladies know she'd been there and done that. She was also a member of the serial marriage club, and even though she projected a who-needs-a-man attitude, somewhere along the line, you could tell she had been kicked in the stomach pretty hard by an all-gone-wrong relationship and a pointy pair of cowboy boots. Her teenage children were giving her problems, she hated her job, she was another one looking for answers to the meaning of life, but she wasn't whiny about it. I got the sense that with Tammy, she came here for something, and she wasn't leaving until she got it. Damn it! She traveled with her nondescript friend, Eileen, but you could tell Eileen was a Tammy wannabe, a shill for Tammy, and just stayed on the sidelines, occasionally lapping up some of Tammy's stardust.

Tammy and I discovered our chakras together, let the vortexes harmoniously speak to our inner selves, and managed to sneak in a few glasses of wine or vodka at night.

I sat cross-legged next to Tammy, that inky black thousand-degree night outside the sweat lodge as we perched ourselves on rocks, waiting for the day to melt into the evening, her gorgeous hot pink sari knotted and wrapped perfectly atop her perky, never-sagging breasts. Kneeling on the ground, we crouched and laid our heads closer to the dirt, whispering, "To all my relations," as we entered the sweat lodge. Yes, the spirits were with us now! With the flap down on the teepee and no air seeping in, nine of us formed a circle around a spirited, roaring fire. Linda, the wife of our leader, a 29-year-old, pot-smoking, long-blond-haired hippie, was in charge of opening the weather-beaten tarp flap every half hour or so, usually when we were all about to pass out, gathering more perfectly formed oval stones from outside of the tent and religiously placing them around the fire. I ended up sitting halfway around the circle, seated on the East of the Eternal Circle of Life. And that spot landed me the coveted job of Cedar Woman. "You are now Cedar Woman. This is a place of honor. The spirits will be with you tonight. The ancestors have picked you, Alexis," the leader told me with all the spiritual reference he could muster. "Great. Oh, this must be a good sign," I thought. I have already won something. I happily took the assignment, hoping for a fast and quicker redemption for all my sins. I felt like I was taking the EZ Pass lane to meet my ancestors. Chanting "to all my relations" again, the mantra of the night, I threw from the small mound of cedar in front of me, each time sending the ancestral flames a little higher and higher inside the teepee and hoping for darkness to reveal light.

Animal possession and connection with the animal spirits was another essential ritual of the sweat lodge experience. Eagles, wolves, buffalo, and lions were the rage for the rest of the group, except me. After another round of beseeching forgiveness and guidance from our ancestors and my cedar-throwing skills becoming more artful, we all inhabited the animals we wanted to become. One by one, each woman chanted, "I am an eagle. I am an eagle." Or, "I am a wolf. I am a wolf." Of course, the spiritual leader was drumming on the floor of the sweat lodge, an Atlanta Braves old Chop Chop Indian beat, while we were all turning into fierce not-to-be-reckoned-with animals. As each woman began chanting, I froze, even in the incinerator of that teepee. At that instant, I was taken back to my second-grade classroom where everyone had to read passages from a book, and I'd count the kids in the rows and seats in front of me, quickly figuring out where my paragraph to read would be and then practiced in my head so I wouldn't sound like an idiot. But this wasn't second grade. "Oh, no, what the hell am I going to be? I can't even think of a fucking animal right now. I can't even think. I must be hallucinating. Maybe I'll be a buffalo," I thought. Then, the mighty buffalo was taken. "I couldn't duplicate an animal, could I?" I wondered to myself.

After the fourth woman sang, "I am a lion. I am a lion," I choked. I couldn't even get that damn Indian chant right, and instead of keeping the pow-wow beat going, I began a slow and steady Jamaican reggae with a hefty dose of rap. Bob Marley and Eminem inhabited my being. Hoping for divine ancestral intervention, the only thing that came out of my mouth was, "I am a dog. I am a dog." That's it. I was a goddamn dog. The Cedar Woman is a dog! Tammy is choking back a muffled laugh. I caught myself. I stopped. I took a deep breath, hoping to catch some random air. I want to know if I will lose weight. I can only hope.

A 10-minute reprieve is offered, and you take it. You are allowed the gift of air, the night, and the stars. The indigo of the evening and the brilliance of the stars seem supernatural, and you are waiting for Carlos Santana to appear, belting out "Black Magic Woman." Your senses are raw, your skin is enveloped with salt, and your throat is parched and scorched. You think you are insane. You sit on the rocks outside the sweat lodge and tell yourself you can do this. You talk to yourself and create a mini dialogue inside your head between the Devil and Jesus. Another vision forming is that of your mom and dad, devout Christians, on their hands and knees at daily mass praying to God that you don't come home like a Jim Jones follower or, worse yet, like a Hari Krishna airport guide.

With one more round of the sweat lodge to go, Tammy and you begin crawling back into the Lilliputian opening of the teepee. Tammy, on all fours, leads the way. "I am sweating my ass off, Tammy. I can't wait until this is over. I don't think I can take much more." You sigh. Before you kiss the ground one last time, offering up this experience to "all my relations," and, frankly, you don't care whose relations are listening at this point, Tammy turns around, stops, looks you in the eye, and in her perfectly pronounced Texan drawl lets out, "Girlfriend, it is sooo damn hot in there, MY IMPLANTS ARE MELTING!!!" Not allowed to break the spiritual experience by speaking, you feel like two deliriously snickering little girls whispering in secret. You invoke Jesus's name several times and pray you don't burn in hell because you crossed over the Catholic line here, but then again, you figure this must be what hell feels like, and you've already gotten a good glimpse by now.

Later, stepping off the plane, dragging your suitcase through the familiar August humidity of Newark, not much cooler than the sweltering Sweat Lodge, you realize—despite the spiritual cleansing, the chanting, the prayers to every relation you've ever known, all your ancestors, and your role as "The Cedar Woman," a title meant for a leader, a healer, someone with wisdom to offer—you could barely guide your way out of your own heartbreak.

And yet . . .

You are not the same woman who arrived in Phoenix.

You did this. You walked into the fire, sat in the heat, let the sweat cleanse something you still can't name. You didn't break. You didn't run. You stayed. You let yourself crack open. And even if you don't have all the answers, even if the ache is still there, you know this much: You are stronger than before.

You are the Cedar Woman.

The world did not change. But you did.

Izzy Forrest-Smith

I'm American
        Small town
                Tax paying
        American

A practicing dyke with both my hands
Read the bible front to back in sunday school
        American

A non-believer,
        But I know Jesus
                lifted four wheel drive
                        Suburban raised
        American

Ask my neighbor for sugar
                Library card owning
                        Vegetable growing
        American

oat milk drinking
                Beef eating
                      Stone cold, Bruce springsteen listening
American

Carhartt wearing
        picked up my meds
                at the Walmart pharmacy
   American

Banned book reading
     Desert wandering
         River swimming
   American

I exist whether you like it or not American
I know this land 'cause I tend to it American
Child of an immigrant American
A queer in every light kind of American
Can't take my joy American
Warm blooded
Art consuming
Riot watching
Hope having
Try and shake the love from me
     American.

Survival

Haya Pomrenze

is a chocolate chip cookie
served by a retired Iraqi Jewess
to a quintet of grenade-toting terrorists,
one of whom wore a smiley face T-shirt.

A mural of Rachel Edri as Rosie the Riveter
covers a large wall in hipster Florentin, Tel-Aviv.
She distracted the terrorists—from fourteen
to twenty hours—depending on who you ask.

The story has become layered, like shawarma
on a spit. Perhaps Rachel served them walnut *kleicha*
in the kitchen, scented by nutmeg and cumin.
And they didn't rest in the salon on newly upholstered furniture.

There is room to believe that she wrapped the wounded
hand of a terrorist, the one with peach-fuzz above his lip.
As the tale unfolds, she may have massaged his forearm,
and spoke to him like a son. It is both disturbing and comforting

that Rachel looks like my dead mother—the same orange
brassy hair, buxom in their ill-fitting floral tops. I imagine this duo
as neighbors, the Lucy and Ethel of Ofakim, yelling
in their thick voices, fighting over who had the best

counter-terrorism baked goods.

Dinosaur Rock

Marsh Rose

Do you remember, when you were three years old, the pet lion that lived with the people next door? You were young. You didn't question how someone could have had a pet lion in your suburban neighborhood. Even years later, when your mother tells you it was just a collie, in your mind's eye you still see its shaggy mane. I have one of those memories too, from my years in Toronto when I was a child. I remember a large flat gray rock that my grandmother kept in the basement. Imbedded in the surface of that rock, wandering diagonally across its face and stepping off over the edge, were the footprints of a dinosaur. I see them in my mind's eye, tracks of a creature about the size of a chicken. They were slender and three-toed, tipped with tiny nails. But unlike your lion, my memory is shared. Someone else also saw that rock. The story came out at a family reunion five years ago. It caused so much trouble, no one ever spoke of it again.

This gathering was at my parents' house in Philadelphia. When I came in via the redeye from San Francisco that morning, I could see that my mother had been preparing for weeks. The hardwood floors shone. Special leaves extended the dining room table to banquet length. Mom had sorted and stacked the good china, and she was in a frenzy of cooking while my father directed from the sidelines. The kitchen was fragrant with the aromas of strudel, borscht, and very good coffee.

Just after noon, an ancient black Buick with Ontario tags lurched to a stop at the curb. My father's two sisters, their husbands, and his younger brother disgorged and milled around on the sidewalk, sorting their luggage and stretching. They had been driving from Toronto since the previous morning. I could hear the throaty, cigarette-cured voice of my Aunt Laika, directing Uncle Vladimir to handle her cosmetics bag with care.

"Pick it up from the bottom. Don't swing it around like that. For Christ's sake, Vlad, you'll get Noxzema all over everything. Give it to me."

Then she charged through the door in an aura of Chanel. Behind her came Aunt Natalie, white-haired and delicate, whose robust laugh takes everyone by surprise. The men remained outside at the curb. I heard them discussing Uncle Vladimir's engine gasket. He thought it was leaking. Uncle Nicolai and Uncle Ivan believed it was condensation caused by the humidity in America.

By early afternoon, everyone had arrived. They came from various highways and airports, from dusty desert towns and teeming old row houses and staid urban brownstones. The men of the older generation grasped one another by the shoulders and stared into each other's eyes. The women wept with emotion and got mascara tracks on their cheeks and sleeves. My sister came in from New Mexico after a two-hour delay in Cleveland and went straight for the vodka. Cousin Alan brought his boyfriend Brooke, who was looking white around the eyes. My cousin Bertha carried her two bad-tempered Chihuahuas in a satchel.

After dinner, we sat around the long table in a tight oval. We ate, we cried, we laughed, we drank Stolichnaya or coffee or both, and we reminisced.

My first cousin Rachel sat opposite me. We began to talk about our childhoods when our extended family lived together in a big brick house in downtown Toronto. Our parents worked while our grandmother babysat Rachel and me, the first born of our generation.

As a special treat, we remembered, Grandmother would take us down to the basement and show us that rock with the dinosaur tracks.

We couldn't remember if our grandmother had found this remarkable object in Russia or if she had inherited it. We agreed, it had always been there in the damp and gloom of the basement, wrapped in a white linen towel with a red border. It was heavy for its size. We recalled that Grandmother was always breathless when she held it out for Rachel and me to take turns stroking its cool surface and tracing the footprints with our small fingers.

Rachel wondered what sort of beast had made the tracks. I had read *Jurassic Park*, so I was the best informed. "I believe it was a baby raptor, maybe even a T-rex, but someone must know," I said. I looked down the table. Uncle Nicolai, on the far end, stirring vodka into his coffee, didn't seem to be embroiled in anything.

"Uncle Nicolai!" I shouted over the cacophony. "What dinosaur made Grandmother's footprints?"

Uncle Nicolai looked up and squinted. "What?"

"You know," I called. "That rock with the dinosaur footprints in the basement in Toronto?"

Uncle Nicolai drew his head back as if he had become farsighted and wanted a better look at me. I heard my parents, sitting across from one another a few seats down the table, ask the person beside them what I was talking about.

"The rock," I said. "Remember? In the basement in Toronto? That rock with the dinosaur tracks? It was on the shelf over the washing machine."

A hush fell over the crowd. Aunt Laika held her coffee cup in midair as if arresting a bird in flight. Aunt Natalie froze in the act of biting into a cheese Danish. Uncle Vlad shuffled his feet and coughed. One by one my family members faced me.

Now unnerved, I said, "I'm asking about Grandmother's rock with the dinosaur footprints that looked like a chicken. It was in the basement."

Aunt Laika rolled her eyes. Uncle Ivan made a circling motion around one ear with an index finger. We sat in silence for what felt like a long time.

Then Rachel spoke. "I wonder what happened to it," she said. "It belonged in a museum."

There was a surreptitious exchange of surprised glances. In retrospect, this covert astonishment makes sense. At the time, Rachel held the reputation as the mentally stable one. She had not yet joined Starchildren of Andromeda and she was still married to an electrical engineer named Barton Carruthers and not yet to Rasta Dwayne.

Slowly, every head turned toward my father, who traditionally sorted out family aberrations. He was frowning down at the table and drawing a triangle on the Damask cloth with his coffee spoon. I saw his chest move as he inhaled and let his breath out. We all waited. Then he shook his head and looked up at Rachel and me.

"Your grandmother was a wonderful woman," he announced and waited until we nodded. "She had the wisdom of a judge and the serenity of a holy person. But she was an uneducated peasant. She was not like you women today with your big educations and fancy careers. She could barely read the newspaper. Even if she could, they never printed about reptiles. Why would they care about reptiles? About the war, certainly, and who died. But your grandmother never went to school and never knew there were dinosaurs. So, with all due respect—"

Aunt Laika interrupted. "Mother grew up on a farm near Omsk, but she went to school before the Revolution."

My father held his palm out toward his sister as if stopping traffic. "Who's telling this, you or me? If you're telling, let me know. I'll be glad to shut up."

Aunt Laika shrugged. "So tell, already." My father turned back to us.

"My mother grew up on a farm near Omsk. Perhaps she went to school before the Revolution." He glanced at his sister. "But she never read a book. No one would have told her about dinosaurs. She had other things to worry about. Now, you are both lovely women. And I admit, I know nothing about the human mind. But you are crazy. Maybe you saw an old potato or a shoe. Your grandmother had no rock, and even if she did, she would not have known what it was."

Aunt Natalie, always the mediator, waved her cheese Danish to get our attention. Our grandmother could make the butcher weep and the chimney sweep clean the furnace, but, she conceded, when it came to extinct lizards, her mother may have been lacking.

"Mother was unconscious about lizards," my father snapped.

Aunt Laika pointed an accusing finger at my father. "Our mother was highly intelligent!"

Dad clapped both hands to his head and looked at the ceiling. "Who's arguing? She was a goddamned genius! She took care of children and cleaned whole chickens including cutting off the head and how to keep the house—"

"And sew! Remember the velvet drapes? She sewed them by hand."

"Where would she have found velvet? It was during the war."

"From a single bone, she could make soup for ten people."

"Do you still have her recipe?"

"I have the one with the kreplach."

"We were poor," Uncle Vlad announced. Heads swiveled. "If she had this rock, why didn't she let us sell it?" He tamped his mustache with his knuckles as he did when deep in thought. "Something like that, dinosaur stuff, what would that be worth? Ten, maybe fifteen hundred dollars?" He was asking Uncle Nik, who was a car salesman and thus familiar with the Capitalist system.

"What, you're saying Mother hid thousands of dollars in the basement while we all starved?"

"We could have fixed the roof!"

"Who's criticizing your mother? God forbid! I'm just asking."

Arguments roared around us until my father struck his coffee cup with his spoon. He would resolve the issue here and now. If his mother had owned this rock, she would have given it to him. He would have known what to do. Why tell only her two tiny granddaughters? And since he, her first-born son, knew nothing about it, that proves it did not exist. Rachel and I were hallucinating.

There was a murmur of assent around the table. Yes, she would have given it to him. Her son would have known what to do. We were hallucinating.

Aunt Natalie and Aunt Laika returned to the velvet drapes issue. My mother got up to start a fresh pot of coffee. I noticed several of my relatives, the older ones, locking eyes, squinting, and then shrugging. Or looking off at a far wall for a moment with brows knitted. Then they would shake their heads and take a long pull of vodka. Tendrils of cigarette smoke rose overhead. Uncle Vlad debated with my father about the horse that pulled the ice wagon to our house in the summers after the war.

Rachel's eyes met mine and we gazed at one another for a long moment. By the way she stirred her coffee, meditatively, in a slow circle, I could tell she was on the fence. Faced with the prospect of becoming embroiled in a family squabble, Rachel could change her entire worldview in a heartbeat. Secretly, I suspected this was the real reason behind her reputation for mental stability.

The weekend moved on. We ate and drank and talked about other things. My father proposed cooking chicken outdoors, but Uncle Vlad dissented in fear of getting tetanus. After a long debate, my father was voted out.

When it was over, we parted with additional rounds of tears and hugs, stayed in touch by phone and letter and email, and we never again discussed the rock. It seemed, by some unspoken mutual decree, an issue better left undisturbed. But I've added a new vignette to those mental images of my childhood.

My grandmother, wearing her apron and with flour on her hands, my only recollection of her, tiptoes out through the back door of the big brick house. She boards a trolley car and travels across town to the University of Toronto. There, she steps up to the podium at the Graduate School of Paleontology and delivers dazzling lectures, in her broken English, about dinosaurs. Then she slips back into the house and takes her place, as we all remember her. In the kitchen. Smiling to herself.

Ode to the Starving Body

Sophie H. Lajnef

As I cast the reflection of my horrid visage onto
the rippling water of the murky lake,
I poke my brown, overgrown nail onto its surface, and watch in awe as
the hideous thing before me is further distorted.

I watch my once-lustrous wings shed, feather by feather, to reveal red,
    pus-filled wounds.
I admire as the deep, infected cuts on my legs bleed and scab, bleed
    and scab, scab and scar.
I run my dirt-caked claws through my greasy hair, interrupted an inch
    from my scalp by matted masses of frizzy, broken hairs, punctuated
    elegantly with ellipses by their split ends.

The wind whispers its most heinous secrets to my flowing, lucious leg
    hairs, combing through them with its sharpest bristles,
And shouts atrocities at my dry, cracked lips, ridden with bulbous,
    stinging cold sores
that ooze a horrible liquid as I smile in admiration at the sight before me.

And as I lean over for a better look, and my wrinkled breasts hang
down to kiss my yellow, calloused toes,
And my bulging stomach hugs my knobby, scraped knees,
And my own ghastly stench impolitely invites itself into my nostrils,

I look myself in my beady eyes,
And whisper to myself in a coarse, grating voice,

"You are a beautiful fucking thing."

Feed her

Jenna A. Smith

the wild places. The desert
      bloom in rocky outcrop
she'll blossom—be hungry again
      to go there againandagain
to find herself a
      rusty red horse, thick with
burrs in mane & tail
      dust settling on lifted levity
prairie verbena—color clustered
      & cupped, she's
on the hunt.
         For sagebrush,
      singing her into desert
folds, she draws water
      from rock, that deep sediment
every time, & every time
      she's sated.

Feed her
that kind of sustenance,
        hard-edged desert dryness
found in parched bones
        bleached white by orbital
heat. She will find
        what marrow remains
suck it dry, bleed it out
        burn ochre onto skin,
put craggy rock to lips
        as tongue skirts sharp edge
takes it in, echoes down
        into her like that
like rimrock canyon.

Swimmer

Barry Fields

Evie had one major ambition before she died—to swim the English Channel. She pulled up YouTube videos for me to watch: women and men tackling the frigid crossing, starting in the dark and fighting the currents. She squeezed my hand and asked me to be at the beach when she came out of the water.

I promised, sorrowful that it would never come to pass. Evie was sick and had a few months to live, but that didn't stop her. She contacted the Channel Swimming Association and made preliminary inquiries about a pilot boat and passport arrangements.

"The Channel's too much," I said. We were sitting on her sofa. "Why don't you scale it back? Do something easier."

"That's not happening."

Evie was nothing if not ferocious. For years, she swam the 400-meter and 800-meter freestyle in US Masters Swimming regional meets. Trophies on a bookshelf testified to her accomplishments. Even now, with metastasized uterine cancer eating away at her vitality, she swam every day she could. To look at her well-toned body and confident manner, you'd never know anything was wrong. She continued working, resolved to live as if nothing were amiss. But there was no way she could train for one of the world's most difficult long-distance swims, let alone complete it.

Evie and I had been a couple for four years, since before her diagnosis. The last thing I wanted was to see her overreaching end in failure, her last days filled with disappointment. I persisted, showing her photographs on my iPad of Lake Tahoe, its stunning green and blue waters surrounded by mountains.

"It's one of the great places in the country for marathon swimmers," I said. "There's a swim they do in the southern part of the lake. Almost eleven miles. It ends at this cool mansion." I showed her pictures of the Vikingsholm, a sprawling Scandinavian-style building, and the heavily forested Emerald Bay where it was located. It would take divine intervention for her to complete the ten and a half miles, around a third of the Channel swim. She needed to come to terms with the limits of her ability.

She took the tablet from me and clicked on several photos with interest.

"It's still probably biting off more than you can chew. It'll be quite a feat given your—" I hesitated. "Your situation."

She handed the iPad back to me after reading about Lake Tahoe's officially recognized long-distance swims, which she'd already heard of. "It's a great idea," she said. "I'll do it as part of my training for the Channel."

It wouldn't have been achievement-oriented Evie if she'd actually agreed to scale back her goal. Graduating from high school as the valedictorian and captain of the girls' swim team got her full university scholarships. At twenty-nine years old, she became the youngest neuropsychologist ever to be on the staff of Massachusetts General Hospital.

I tried to prepare myself for losing her, but it was impossible when she had so much life in her. I longed to comfort her, but couldn't get past her wall of self-sufficiency.

In the winter she turned thirty, Evie went for another round of chemo and radiation, telling no one but me and forbidding me to visit her. Well-wishers and their bouquets of flowers required payment: thank-you cards, expressions of appreciation, phone calls. Evie owed nothing to anyone and intended to keep it that way.

I spent the three to four days of her hospitalizations imagining her isolated and miserable, sick from the treatments. A psychologist at another Boston hospital, I took the day off as soon as I knew she was back from the final one. I went to her third-floor condo in Brighton. We'd never lived together because she considered it an infringement on her autonomy. Although I had a key, I hadn't told her I'd be dropping by, and I rang the bell.

I waited, and when she answered I could hear she was right on the other side of the door. "Who's there?"

"Brian."

"What are you doing here?"

"You can use the company. Let me in."

The door unbolted with a snap. When I opened it, she was walking slowly to her bed, hunched over like an old woman with the energy drained out of her. She got under the covers and scowled at me, an issue of *Swimmer* magazine next to her. The place had a welcoming, cozy feel, with full-length curtains, potted plants, and a bed quilt with flowers inside circles.

"You shouldn't come uninvited," she said.

I didn't feel welcome now. "I brought you a sandwich. Roast beef on rye, cole slaw on the side." I put the bag on a tray and placed it on her bed.

"Thank you. Now please go away."

She pushed the tray away and pointed to the door. Instead of leaving, I walked to the kitchen and got her a bubbly water from the fridge. I sat on the bed. "Eat."

"I'm not hungry."

"You want to do a big swim? Eat. You're so skinny." Over the past few months, it looked like she'd lost ten to fifteen pounds she didn't have to spare.

She turned away, gazed out the window, and sighed loudly. "Just go."

Evie's pale face had a tired, worn look. She disliked my seeing her bald head and had put on a beanie before coming to the door.

When I stayed overnight, she wouldn't take it off until the lights were out.

"You don't have to be alone just because you feel bad."

"Don't you understand? I know you mean well, but I don't want you here. Not when I'm like this."

She didn't touch the sandwich and wouldn't say another word. After several minutes I reluctantly walked to the door. "Let me know when you want me to come back."

A few days later, she'd recovered enough that we went to a restaurant and a movie like any ordinary couple. Evie smiled, chatted easily, held my hand as we walked, and kissed me spontaneously. In our lovemaking that night I felt her hunger for connection. She said she loved me, which I'm sure she did.

The breeze ruffled Lake Tahoe, and morning sunlight bounced off the water in silver flashes. The mountains rising from the shoreline had lost all their snow, and the deep green of mountain conifers covered the slopes. The city itself at the southern tip of the lake was unattractive, but the affordable Hotel Azure gave us a comfortable room overlooking the pool. From our balcony, I watched Evie swim laps for a half hour the afternoon we arrived. Looking at her smooth stroke, the straight-arm freestyle she planned to use for her long-distance swim, it was tempting to imagine she was well, and pleasurable to imagine her having the endurance to cross from France to England.

In August the water was at its warmest, although still cold. We woke up early for Evie's swim, which could take up to eight hours. We picked up our powerboat after an early breakfast at Red Hut Cafe, where Evie ate a healthy meal for once. She was about to need it.

The boat cost over a thousand dollars for the day. Evie insisted on paying the whole thing herself, just like she did the hotel room and car rental. The only expense I had was my plane ticket to Reno.

She was too weak to be attempting such a feat, but try telling her that. The last few weeks hadn't been bad, but the cancer was still destroying her insides, sapping her stamina, slowly annihilating everything but her will. When she gave up in the middle of the lake, she would have to realize the English Channel was unattainable.

We motored up to Cave Rock, the standard starting point of the swim on the Nevada side eleven miles away, just a hair over the distance she was about to attempt on her own steam. Evie sat beside me, barely talking. "Unbelievable," she said. I didn't know if she meant the lake and mountains, or the fact that she was undertaking her first marathon swim. She stood up as I slowed down for our approach to the boat launch, the official starting point. A jumbled rock jetty was on one side of the wooden dock and a rocky headland on the other.

Evie stripped down to her bathing suit, a light two piece, and put on her bathing cap, goggles in her hand. Even though we were alone on an informal swim, Evie demanded we follow the rules, just like those for the Channel; once in the water, she could touch neither me nor the boat, even when I handed her something to eat.

I cut the motor and held onto the fence, expecting her to jump out. But she didn't. She sat down again and let out a groan. She slid off the seat and onto the floor of the boat, lying on her back, eyes wide to the sky.

"Please, God, not now. Not here." Her voice came out as a whispered prayer.

Evie had never let me see her suffer. When she felt pain coming on, she sent me away, her anger mounting quickly if I hesitated. Most of us want a loved one there when we're in pain. We want reassurance, our hand held. Not her. To hear her tell it, she'd been like that as a child, ever since losing her mother at ten years old to the same cancer Evie was battling.

Her abdomen swelled up rapidly, ballooning from the flat belly of an underweight athlete to the roundness of a six-months-pregnant woman. My own gut turned queasy at the sight. I pulled out my phone. "I'm calling 911."

"No. Don't."

She lay moaning on the floor of the boat, which rocked and slapped gently against the dock bumper. The sight of her, reduced to a helplessness she hid from the world, was pitiful.

Evie began to cry, which I'd never seen her do before. She reached out her hand and I took it, feeling as powerless and worried as she looked.

"It hurts so much," she said.

"I'm here." It was all I could think of to say.

I knelt beside her, my knees against the hard fiberglass bottom of the boat. Her eyes closed, her breathing shallow, a low moan escaped her with each exhale. A strange serenity came over me, and I observed her with benevolent compassion, as if from a distance. I put my hands on her swollen abdomen and closed my eyes. For a few seconds I did nothing more, only felt the taught skin and its slight movement with her labored breathing.

I have no explanation for it, but a white light appeared. It was above me, a blazing, shapeless intensity that descended and entered my head. As soon as it did, I knew exactly what I had to do. I pictured the light channeled by my body, streaming down through my arms and out my hands. I remained perfectly still, my breathing steady. With my eyes closed, I saw the light beaming out my fingers like lasers, penetrating Evie's abdomen.

It grew more intense, like the unbearable light of the sun, pouring from above, coursing through me into the woman I loved. My hands were producing enormous heat, which I thought must be my imagination until Evie whispered, "It's burning. It's burning. So hot."

A bolt of lightning struck from above, a quick, jagged flash that in an instant traversed my body into hers. Although I didn't move a muscle, Evie screamed.

I removed my hands. As quickly as her abdomen had expanded, it contracted. Flat once more. Evie sat up.

"What did you do?"

"Nothing," I said. "I don't know what happened. It didn't come from me."

She looked at me, perplexed, distrustful. "You did something."

I had no response. I'd felt more like the receiver than the generator. Now that it was over, it frightened me. Was there really some power out there I had tapped into, that used me as a conduit? How did it make the swelling go away?

We sat in silence a good two minutes. The boat had drifted away from the dock, and we were floating in the cove. An SUV pulling a boat up drove into the parking area and was getting into position to launch it.

"What do you want to do?" I asked.

"Swim," she said.

It took over seven hours for Evie to touch the shore of Emerald Bay. "You're incredible," I said. "To do this in the state you're in."

She dried herself with the oversized bath towel she'd brought from home. "I knew I was going to make it as soon as I started. I felt it. The strength in my arms. The way I was breathing."

The Nordic mansion sprawled along the shoreline, all stone and red-tiled roof, but Evie was too exhausted to go for a tour. Out on the open water, she changed out of her wet suit into dry clothes. In her stunning success, her compact body radiated a soundness I hadn't sensed from her in years. But she was quiet, barely speaking. For most of the ride she faced forward in the bow, and when she looked back at me, it was warily, as if I were a stranger.

Her withdrawal continued on the way to Reno and in the airport. In her place, I would have been babbling, overjoyed to be with my partner after a great adventure. I asked what was wrong, and she said nothing. She read a book on the plane, distant, inaccessible, while I squirmed uneasily. You couldn't push Evie, the most headstrong person I'd ever known. She'd talk about whatever was bothering her in her own time.

When Evie felt well, we saw each other two or three times during the work week, having dinner and spending the night together before rushing off to our respective hospital jobs. Now, she didn't return my calls or texts for an anxiety-ridden week. Something was wrong. I knew better than to believe she'd been basking in the triumph of crossing of the lake. She'd probably only reported it to friends from the swimming club.

When she finally got in touch, she wanted to meet at a coffee shop. Troubling.

I arrived first, claimed a table in the morning weekend rush, and waited with a big knot in my stomach. Evie saw me, nodded, and went up to the counter. She sat across from me with her latte and a muffin. No kiss hello. I reached my hand across the table, and she withdrew hers. She looked at me without speaking for several seconds with an expression of calm resolve. I knew before she said a word that she'd gone to a place beyond my reach.

"I had a bunch of tests this week," she said. She tore off a piece of muffin, put it in her mouth.

She must have bad news, I thought. In spite of the inexplicable episode in the boat, her health had gone downhill. She was about to tell me she was dying.

I was wrong.

"My white blood count was normal. Red cells, too."

"That's great."

"The CA-125 test showed there's no tumor anymore. They biopsied several lymph nodes. They were all clear. I had an MRI that my oncologist said was impossible."

"I don't understand," I said.

"I don't have cancer anymore. It's gone. I'm in full remission."

"That's terrific. Why are you so glum?"

She ate more of her muffin, drank her coffee thoughtfully, and took a long time to answer. "I don't know how you did it, but it was you. You put your hands on me like some sort of faith healer. You zapped me with your magic energy. Right there in that boat, I knew the cancer was gone. I could feel it."

The incident on the boat had shaken me, but this was freaky, incomprehensible. "The only thing that came from me was love. For you. Magic energy? I don't believe in that kind of stuff. I don't know what happened."

"It was you," she said again. "You cured me."

The cafe was packed. One fellow read a magazine by himself, but the breakfast crowd sat at the other tables in twos, threes, and fours in animated conversations. Evie and I spoke loudly to hear each other over the din.

"I don't think so. But even if I did, so what? Aren't you grateful it's over?"

"I don't want to be grateful to you. You healed me. Now I'm in your debt. I'll always be in your debt."

Fiercely independent Evie never permitted people to help her outside of impersonal, paid professionals. She had friends she'd never told about her medical issues. She had pushed me away every time I offered assistance.

"You don't owe me anything," I said.

"My life. I owe you my life. I feel awkward just talking to you. Beneath you."

"No way. Let it go."

Evie had been maintaining a stern expression, but stared into her emptying coffee mug before considering me impassively. "I can't live with that. Don't you see, Brian? I can't be around you anymore."

My head was spinning as though I'd entered a surreal space. Although I tried, no argument of mine could make her change her mind.

After Evie broke up with me, I went through months of mourning. I'd lost her as surely as if illness had taken her. I had my work, my friends, and when a year passed, I met someone else. Wendy was a graphic artist who designed web-based ads for high-profile companies. She was tall and lanky and got me out of the gym and into the White

Mountains of New Hampshire. We spent a number of weekends at a B&B, hiking the trails.

I told Wendy about Evie, of course, everything except what happened on the boat and the real reason she'd left me. In fact, I never told anyone. If someone had spun a story like that, I would have dismissed it as nonsense. My hands looked and felt normal. I experimented when my sister came down with the flu. No supernatural force emanated from me.

Wendy subscribed to the *Boston Globe* online. We'd been together a year when she handed me her laptop and pointed to an article. The American Cancer Society was sponsoring Evie in a fund-raising swim of the English Channel. Over two thousand swimmers had made the crossing, but Evie was the first advanced cancer survivor. Vertex Pharmaceuticals was paying all her expenses including a support team. Other businesses had already pledged donations for cancer research.

Even though I hadn't spoken to her in nearly two years, I had to see Evie when she emerged from the water, as she'd asked me to do.

"I think you're still in love with her," Wendy said.

"There's some lingering affection maybe. But the bond isn't there. I love you and only you. Evie was difficult. You could only get so close to her, then she'd put up a wall. She did it with everyone. Ending our relationship was the best thing she could have done for me."

Evie planned to start on the French side at Cap Gris-Nez, so in August Wendy and I took a vacation in England. We spent a few days in London, toured Cornwall, and hiked along its rugged coast. Before returning to Heathrow, we drove to Dover and walked down to the base of Shakespeare's Cliff to wait for Evie.

The Channel presented obstacles the lake hadn't. Swimmers had to dodge ocean-going freighters. Icy water, strong tides, and bad weather reduced the chances of success for the most fit marathoner to under 50 percent. Then there were the jellyfish. After Wendy and I got there, a call came from Evie's support craft that she'd been stung and had to stop.

With all the publicity, a large crowd had gathered on the beach below the cliff. Conversation came to a halt. My first thought, when I saw the crestfallen faces of the Vertex and American Cancer Society execs, was how crushed Evie would be. Even when she was sick, she'd been certain she would succeed. Now a mindless marine invertebrate had ruined it for her.

I couldn't bear to see Evie step off the boat in defeat. "Let's go," I said.

I turned away, but Wendy grabbed my arm and pointed to the Cancer Society rep. He put the microphone to his mouth and made an announcement over the loudspeaker. "Evie hasn't touched the boat. She's refusing help."

I squeezed Wendy's hand. The fellow put his phone to his ear, then spoke again. "She says she's going to continue."

Reporters' video cameras caught the crowd clapping and cheering. We waited. A helicopter whirred overhead and out over the water, and sometime later the Cancer Society rep broadcast excitedly, "She's coming."

I held my breath as I scanned with my binoculars. The bow of the boat bobbed up and down. A man was looking over the side, but the chop of the water hid Evie. The excitement among the spectators grew palpable and the buzz of conversation increased. An hour later I saw her, one arm reaching out, then the other, stroke after stroke, legs kicking steadily.

She touched bottom, stood, and walked out of the water. Her skin had a healthy sheen, and she looked robust and buoyant through her exhaustion. The spectators clapped and cheered again. Evie took the mic and gave a short speech, thanking everyone who had helped, urging people to donate to the Cancer Society, and praising Vertex for its novel approaches to medical treatment. There were so many people I didn't think she noticed me. Wendy and I were about to leave when she approached.

"Hello, Brian."

"Hello yourself. Congratulations. You did it." I resisted the impulse to hug her and introduced her and Wendy.

"Thank you both for coming," Evie said. And to me, "I never thought you'd be here. It's a nice surprise."

Three years later Evie left a voice message to call her. I hadn't thought about her in some time. Wendy and I had married by then, and she was expecting. All Evie would tell me when we talked was that she had another swim to do and needed to see me. She asked me to meet her at her condo.

Her place looked pretty much the same. She had a new sofa, which I sat on, and there were framed photographs of her English Channel swim grouped on a wall. She served herbal tea. After a few preliminaries, I asked her what she planned on swimming.

"I'm going to swim around Kauai. No one's ever done it." The island was so large it would take three days, coming out of the water each night. Her first stage would be along the Na Pali coast from Princeville to Nohill Point.

"You never lacked for ambition. What does it have to do with me?"

"The cancer came back. They say five years in remission and you're as good as new. I almost made it."

"Evie, I'm so sorry."

Advanced tumors had been found in her lungs, another in a breast. Cancer had spread to the thigh bone. As the news sank in, I thought back to our time together. Not just the frustration of her keeping me at arm's length from her struggles against disease, but the good times, too. The movies we'd spend hours dissecting, dinner parties with friends, concerts, and Patriots games. My feelings for her had faded, but I remembered how we'd snuggle and her solemnity when she would tell me she loved me.

"They want me to start chemo again. Vertex has some new treatments they're going to let me try. But the truth is, I don't plan on going through it again."

"What choice do you have? It's not like you to give up."

"That's why I called you. So you can do what you did before. Put your hands on me and get God to throw a thunderbolt at you or something."

"What?" My hand shook so violently I spilled hot tea on myself. "That's impossible."

"It was impossible before."

I put my cup on the coffee table and stood up. "It was a fluke. I told you then it wasn't something I controlled."

"Just do whatever you did the first time."

Her calm assurance agitated me. I began pacing, went over to the window and looked out onto the street. A woman was walking her dog, and a man was pushing a baby carriage.

I turned back to her. "Maybe something clicked because we were so entwined. You were my life." To touch her breast and thigh with comfort involved an intimacy we no longer shared. "What was between us is gone," I added.

"I think all you need is the intention. You can do it."

"No. It was a one-time thing. It never happened again."

"Did you try?"

"Twice. It didn't work. With someone I love, too."

She shot me an accusatory look, as if I were lying or purposely withholding a gift, but my tension was enough to block whatever had passed through me at Lake Tahoe.

"Maybe along with what you did before, the experimental treatments will work," I said.

"I'm not going to find out."

A month later, I learned that Evie had quit her job and gone to Hawaii. An act of finality, as if she didn't expect to return. I began looking online through *The Garden Island*, a local Kauai newspaper, and two weeks later found an article, "Boston Swimmer to Attempt Island Circumnavigation." Evie in her bathing suit was coming out of the water at a beach giving the thumbs-up sign. The writer explained that the Na Pali coast Evie aimed to tackle her first day had strong tides and unpredictable currents that could pull swimmers off course and slam them into hidden rocks and reefs along coastal cliffs. An unofficial tally placed the number of dead swimmers there at over 80. The article quoted Evie: "They say it's impossible. I'm going to prove them wrong." The article ended with a statement from the coach of a Kauai swim club: "Nobody swims there. Nobody. You get caught in a current sweeping you towards the shore, no boat's coming after you. You're a gonner."

As her condition deteriorated, Evie would become incapacitated, fed intravenous morphine to manage unbearable pain before the disease killed her. Not a future Evie would allow. I realized that with its multiple risks, conquering Kauai's coast wasn't her main goal. Hers was an act of defiance, a way of claiming victory whether she made *Guinness World Records* or her body washed up months later on the shores of Japan. This was the Evie who would exist to the end, determined and unstoppable, taking charge of her life in her last big swim.

Satisfying a Woman

Jennifer Schollars

"I don't know what I'm running toward. Or from?" I spoke these words, dryly, to a woman I met on a dating app last January. She told me immediately she doesn't see a romantic future with me, but we kept seeing each other anyway. Sitting in a creperie together months later and over two hundred miles away from home, my first-date-with-a-woman turned platonic lesbian friend stared at me and my half of the gluten-free crepe we split.

"Jenny, maybe now it's just about living," she said between sips of water from a plastic cup. "That's it. You've spent the last ten years living for two people. Now, maybe you just live for yourself." Her response stuck with me stronger than the mud my boots picked up on our hike in the Ozarks.

As it turned out, opening a private therapy practice wasn't the only risk I'd take in my twenty-eighth year. Life offered an answer to a question I didn't know I asked and extended the possibility of a new life. I accepted. After being married to a man for seven years, I came out as lesbian, got divorced, and moved into my own apartment before I could celebrate a single year of knowing I was gay. I threw a housewarming party, where I received a lavender-colored apron with the outlines of my two cats' faces on the front pockets, hand-embroidered by a friend I met in ballet class that summer. I hung wicker sconces in my living room, organized my closet by sleeve length and color, and neatly layered my clothing into the three dresser drawers my ex-husband once stuffed to the brim. I hung a painting of a swan above my small, black folding leaf table, and placed one of my own collages, framed, above my kitchen sink. My life in November looked entirely different than in January of the same year—a wonderful and terrifying thing.

The uncovering of my sexuality granted both a second lease on life and an existential crisis. Before coming out, I thought I knew myself and where I was going. I pursued two degrees, left a religion, and moved to a city large enough to support public transportation. I pictured an entire life with my ex-husband, growing old together and taking Polaroids on New Year's Eve. Writing the year with a sharpie and sliding the photo into a clear, plastic album. Us, buying a home with a backyard garden—one with string lights and a pebbled patio to drink coffee together in the mornings and chamomile tea alone at night. I pictured a life visiting daycares before choosing between my paycheck and a Montessori education for my unborn child, and I left Saturday morning ballet classes wondering if they might love ballet too, or despise it.

"You worried about having kids?" my ex asked two months after we broke up while sitting on the cat-scratched couch my parents bought us as their wedding gift.

"No. I don't want kids," I answered immediately. The shocked look on his face confirmed what I wasn't yet sure I'd heard correctly from my own mouth. As it turns out, being a wife to a man and a parent were two things I only expected to enjoy because everyone told me I would.

I confronted the narrative of who I am versus who others expected me to be, daily. Though, I wasn't a new visitor to the idea. Three years earlier, I led a therapy group for adults in recovery from substance use disorders. We gathered around a glossy, brown conference table, where I sat at the head wearing bright yellow jeans, a black sweater, and a bumble-bee headband I bought online for

Halloween night. "I'm a thera-bee," I told the group. Group members, dressed in Cookie Monster footed pajamas and band T-shirts from the eighties, appreciated my efforts. They offered me warm smiles and a piece of the pizza they bought on break while I was busy looking for dry-erase markers that were a little less dry. I declined, though I noted their generosity. That night, I asked members to create two columns: one for the expectations placed on them by society, and one for self-chosen expectations. I encouraged dialogue within the group, exploring life narratives, where they come from, and how they can support or destroy us. I should have completed the exercise myself before giving it to the group. I didn't. I have now.

Gaining more than an early mid-life crisis before thirty, I also found a therapist. "Write down three to five moments you've felt satisfied in your life," she said. "They don't need a story or an arc, just a moment."

"Okay. I can do that." Though I agreed to the homework, I walked out of her office at three o'clock and sat in my car, waiting for the engine to warm, wondering if I'd ever felt satisfied. I spent the next two weeks writing and erasing possible moments of satisfaction in my phone's overcrowded notes app. I compiled a short list ranging from a cool, spring breeze on an April morning, felt through the crack of an open sliding glass door, to accepting the outstanding philosophy student award at graduation—one handed to me by the same college professor who said, "Oh, you don't want to sit in here with us boys talking about philosophy. The education department is down the hall." Being chosen by the department chair and then handed the award by philosophy boy embodied some kind of satisfaction.

I downloaded two dating apps in December and discovered my circle of friends also married men young enough to avoid online dating. I sat alone one night on my newly delivered, green, velvet couch and carefully chose five photos. One of me smiling in a coffee shop, another brushing my hair out of my face in the spring, one hiking in Utah, one taken during a ballet intensive wearing my favorite pink, floral leotard, and one with my beloved cat, Picasso. Three of the five photos were taken by my ex-husband, but only I would know that.

Before posting my profile, I Googled the definitions for "long-term relationship" and "life partner," after feeling confused by the many relationship options I could select and multi-select. Eventually, with both of my cats vying for warmth in the space between my outstretched legs, I posted my profile for women to swipe right or left. After a couple of months, I felt emboldened. When I matched, I reached out first. I was picky about who I liked on the apps. Not wanting children, nor fond of smoking cigarettes, plus ruling out anyone whose job description was "CEO bitch" or had an answer to a prompt like, "dating me is like gaslighting," I learned to navigate telling women I was once married to a man. Some women unmatched immediately, others stopped responding after a few messages.

I learned dating apps had an entire culture, and that both nineteen- and forty-seven-year-old women were particularly fond of my profile, though I hadn't set my age range that widely. After attending a mediocre coffee date, I decided a relationship was something I wanted, but not something I felt desperate to find. Swiping, matching, chatting, didn't contribute much to my daily life. Though, I continued on the apps, hoping I would eventually build a bridge from, "I have two cats. How about you?" to a true connection.

For 14 days between appointments with my own therapist, I made it my mission to explore satisfaction. I read about the link between gratitude and overall life satisfaction, and I imagined them sitting closely together in a thought cloud holding hands. I revisited Buddhist teachings on equanimity and listened to podcasts on hedonism and nihilism. Twice, my own clients sat across from me in my office, just beyond the fiddle leaf fig losing leaves because I'd yet to repot it, vocalizing similar concerns in their lives. They questioned what path they were on and how they'd know when they were heading in the right direction. They weren't aware, of course, I'd already wondered that for myself earlier in the afternoon. And the one previous.

On a late February morning, I opened the living room window of my one-bedroom apartment. I listened to the birds and their daily gossip and ate eggs and toast and coffee. My cats napped, bellies up, on a heating pad I bought two years earlier. I smiled. Then, sliding my pale legs into hiking shorts for the first time in months, my feet into mud-covered boots, and my equally pale arms into an over-pilled sweatshirt I bought on clearance in college at a thrift store, I drove thirty minutes to a hiking trail. On a whim.

I hiked at my own pace, pausing along with my podcast, to view the overhead train race past me, rhythmically clicking and banging before disappearing. The late winter snowmelt crunched and squashed beneath my boots, loosening the hardened mud I set out with. I passed only a few others—they, too, enjoying the liminal space between late winter and early spring. With the sun pouring over me like a warm wash of liquid on the back of my neck, I kept my hands inside my pockets, realizing that was the trick for keeping my body temperature balanced.

I wondered how I'd fill my afternoon. No one expected me at home. No one cared if I skipped making the chicken salad today because I wanted leftover curry for lunch instead. My apartment was already clean because I left it that way. I had friends to call, should I feel lonely, and one with a newborn who welcomed an iced coffee and a drop-in anytime I offered. I had complete freedom. After a steep incline and a long stretch of gravel, I sat on a weathered bench beneath a tree, not to rest, but to befriend Satisfaction for as long as she wished to stay.

Second Career

Noel Plennert Poston

She used to study desert rats,
then became a nurse.
She said rats, like men,
tend to tunnel far
and fast.
She watched them
from her tent, took notes
into the nights.

Now she turns men over,
as she turns the soil
in her garden, works
her fingers into furrows,
loosens clods
of withered muscle.

So many years she's felt
her way along the wards
of barren flesh and bone.
She prefers the dirt,
within her own beds now—
Potent, rich with rot.

One time I watched her dig
a trench,
shovelful by shovelful,
cover roots laid bare,
soiled bodies stripped
by wind and time.

I would see her stop to squint
into the sun, then
toss her head and laugh.
At what?
Her boots were always caked with muck.

A sheen of sweat, her face
and arms aglow. She worked
after the sun gave out.
She would not wash
her hands until she went
to bed alone.

I watched her plant potatoes,
split rock and build a shed.
She could cry and work,
and carry on,
sort seed and bend
for hours on end,
thin the finest row
of radishes.

I never saw her trap
or kill a garden pest
or harm a man.
At the end of the day,
she kept to her way,
faithful to her
companion,
work.

Yesterday's News

Amy Haddad

The nurses wasted nothing. They stocked
their black bags with papers; the headlines
from the day before, on their way out
the door whatever the weather,
on foot to their home visits.

The papers, unfolded over dinner
tables, or sometimes, Singer sewing machine
stands, kept the surface clean but not sterile.
On top of obituaries and grocery store ads

the nurse laid down her supplies—
tape, scissors, gauze, alcohol, iodine,
a bottle of water, soap, and towels
in case the house lacked plumbing
or the well water was brown.

Debris from the nurse's handiwork—
soiled dressings, afterbirth, spent stitches
were wrapped in newsprint packages
like fish bones or potato peels
to be dumped in the trash.

Newspapers were laid on dirt floors, beds,
or chairs, a barrier to protect the nurse
from insects and filth that could not be swept
away. Families often turned their heads
while the nurse sat on the paper
and took out her pen to take notes.

Into the Blue

Shakira Croce

Free, my body
learns to ride the current.
Aqua hues swell and
lift me back to shore.
But my friend never came
out past the breaking waves.
I didn't understand why,
and she didn't offer a reason.
Could she be content wading in the shallows
waiting for my return?
We sit together for hours patiently packing sand,
molding giant walls for our castle
before it's swallowed by the tide.
I was older when I realized as I climbed
into the inflatable house with the other mothers:
they never taught most girls to swim.
I wonder if she ever left the certainty
of her family's island, the constant threat
of swells and storms.
I teach my daughter to scale the air-filled tower,
the trick of choosing which foot to place first.
I lift her limbs over and over
until she alone, like a redwood
is grand enough
no matter what quakes beneath the surface
to unfurl herself skyward into the blue.

Rainforest Fermata

Ayla Gard

I

The buzzing heat of Amazonia, a place so thick with so many heartbeats a mind can't comprehend just how alive it really is. A living basin, where four months after I meet the naturalist, and four miles from the equator, we push through palm leaves toward the Rio Aguarico and its pebbled river beach, in the middle of the world, in the middle of some three million square miles of rainforest. We're at the back of his family's property and we're going to set up a campsite on the bank above the water, then clamber down to swim before the sun sets.

Leaves rustle nearby and I wonder if there are dangerous animals in this part of the rainforest. I suppose from the forest's perspective, I'm the dangerous animal. But here, there might also be jaguars and peccaries, bush dogs and bushmaster snakes. It doesn't hurt to be cautious. When I ask the naturalist, he promises me that we won't see any large animals; most have been hunted from this area. But, like always, he reminds me that if there are any, they will likely see us.

The animal on my mind, although I don't want to say its name out loud in case I summon it, is the Amazonian bushmaster. It's a nocturnal pit viper, sometimes growing to 12 feet long, with skin the texture of pineapple. It's one of the most venomous snakes in the world, up there with the inland taipan in Australia, where I'm from. The scary thing about the bushmaster, though, is that it chases people who annoy it. The naturalist told me a story about his dad hunting in the forest, back when their community was still allowed to hunt in the forest. His dad had been going after a wild pig, not realizing that a bushmaster was also going after the same pig, and, dinner plans foiled, the giant snake had turned its focus to the man and chased him through the forest.

"What would happen if we see one?" I ask the naturalist, but he doesn't reply.

"What would happen if we tread on one?" I press, but he is silent as he holds out his hand to help me hop across stones in a creek that sings freshwater songs.

It is a lesson I have learned over and over from him, on this trip into the jungle and the others before it. And it is one he will teach me over and over again: to listen not to the thoughts that wander to future places, but to the stories we are being told in every moment.

II

Floating in a lagoon, my first trip into the Amazon, the moon rose fat above the darkened canopy below a constellation-lit sky. We were only two days into our story then, the naturalist and me, and we climbed back into the canoe, wet and shivering in the cool air. That was the first time we kissed, not one person or another leaning in but both of us just sort of falling into each other, and I got that feeling that comes along with a person every so often, not with every person but with some, that feeling of being home, though I didn't know if it was him that felt like home or the rainforest, as though they were separate.

We didn't stay out there long. When we looked up, the boat was drifting close to the mangroves where anacondas and caimans surely moved through the water. The naturalist rowed us back to the lodge, through the narrow shallow channels where birds slept in the branches. Wanting to avoid the sound of footsteps on the wooden boardwalk, and the sensor lights that would illuminate all the bamboo villas if we walked past one, he hoisted me onto his back—the damp of his neck on my check, one of his hands gripping mine to his chest—and carried me across the edge of the grass to the villa where my Brazilian coworker and friend, Anna, was still sleeping. We'd come into the jungle together at the tail end of a work trip in another part of the Amazon; here, the naturalist was teaching us and two other couples about Indigenous plant wisdom and how to survive in the jungle.

In the morning over breakfast in the dining room, monkeys chattered in the forest behind us, and I waited for Anna to say something about me coming in late, but she didn't seem to have noticed that I'd left, more focused on her coffee. The naturalist appeared and sat at the other end of the breakfast table, long black hair pulled into a ponytail.

"Good morning," he said, and didn't make eye contact.

Anna's eyes had brightened on something across the dining room. "There's a monkey!" she said.

It was an adorable thing, clambering along the banister at the edge of the dining area, small body the color of cappuccino. It looked like it was wearing a fuzzy white motorcycle helmet, dark eyes peeking through the center.

"That's a white-fronted capuchin," the naturalist said.

"Is it looking for food?" I asked.

"Yes, probably looking for fruit."

"But we can't feed it, right?" I wanted to give it some of the papaya on my plate, but I knew that we weren't supposed to feed the wildlife.

The naturalist sucked his teeth. "Another lodge used to feed these monkeys, years ago. Then one day the monkeys broke in and took all the fruit of the kitchen."

Anna laughed. "What happened to them?"

"They stopped feeding them, and the monkeys spent four days crying and complaining," he said. "Now they travel around through different lodges, about eight of them in a group."

"It's the same monkeys that stole the fruit?" I asked, wondering if we've just encountered a member of the original fruit gang. The capuchin is gone now, swinging through some trees next to the lodge.

"Yes, there's one dominant male that leads the group around. His job is to distract the enemies so the rest of the group can get away."

This is a good job for a man, I thought.

Once we'd recovered from the excitement of seeing a real-life monkey gang leader up close, the naturalist explained the plans for the day. We'd be taking the boat over to visit one of the Indigenous communities that lived in the reserve, where we'd eat lunch. Then we'd come back and do a night hike, to look for nocturnal animals like scorpions, some frogs, and maybe kinkajou on the canoe ride back, if we were lucky. I couldn't remember what a kinkajou was exactly, but pictured a cute nocturnal mammal with round ears and little bulging spheres for eyes.

Later that morning we took a long canoe ride to the community, a clearing in the forest along the river with a thatched roof open-air structure in front of scattered houses, flowering shrubs, and roaming chickens. The fragrant smell of the white-flowered quinine tree and wood smoke from a small fire drifted on the hot air. Here we'd be making tortillas de yucca.

Our host led us out to a small clearing where she showed us how to pull the yucca from the earth. She showed us a plant ready for harvest, explaining in Kichwa, which the naturalist translated, that once the yucca roots were ready, you could preserve them underground for up to three years before harvesting.

"Who wants to try pulling it out?" she said, wiping the dirt from her hands onto an embroidered cotton dress.

Anna wrapped her hands around the thickest stem of the plant and pulled. It didn't budge.

"You try," she said to me.

I grabbed the stem and pulled, and the earth lifted around it and my hands chafed, but I could not get the plant out. It seemed to not want to disconnect from the earth.

Finally, someone in our group got it, stumbling back as the tubers uprooted from the ground in a spray of dirt to breathe their first air. Our host removed the stem with a cutlass and dusted the dirt off the sweet potato–looking things, gathering them up to take back to the hut where we'd wash them, grate them, grind them into tortillas to cook them on a clay frying pan over fire.

On the way back to the hut the naturalist and I were talking, and I realized at some point that we were walking so slowly we'd lost the rest of the group. Out of sight and next to a flowering guava tree, he grabbed my hand. I looked down at my hand and back up at him, and for a second it seemed that the cicadas and the birds in the small farm around us and the jungle beyond had all gone silent and time stood still.

Right in that moment, tiny nerve endings in my hand told a pea-sized gland at the back of my neck to dispatch chemical messengers toward my brain, the same chemical messengers that lie dormant in a poppy seed, and these strings of opiate molecules curled around the pain receptors and quietened them. We feel good, they told my brain, we feel euphoric. It was the same feeling I would feel later that night, when on our night hike, the naturalist would ask everyone to turn off their flashlights and their phone lights and stand still in the dark to listen to the sounds around us, and he would take one step back toward me and find my hand in the dark, hold it for a whole minute, and I would be so focused on hearing my heartbeat in my hand that I would not hear the night jungle sounds, the crickets or the potoos or the kinkajou.

Earlier that day in the field, he kissed me again and I laughed and looked around him to see if anyone was watching us, but no, the group had definitely moved on. I was nervous that if Anna came back looking for me and found me kissing our guide, I'd never hear the end of it.

"I wanted to do that all morning," he said.

A few nights later, our last in the jungle, I told Anna I was going to meet the naturalist after dinner.

"I knew something was going on," she said. "I swear you two are going to have babies together."

He and I lay in a hammock down below the lodge. We talked about our families, our love for plants. I held up his hand, our fingers interlaced.

"How did you get that scar on your thumb?" I asked him.

"Piranha bite," he said.

I laughed. "How did you really get it?"

"I'm serious. I was fishing for piranhas."

"Wait, you can eat piranhas? Do they taste good?"

"Not as good as other fish, like arapaima, catfish, Amazonia salmon. But people eat it if there's nothing else available."

"How big are they?"

He held up his hands, measuring about a foot of space between them. I realized I'd never given a lot of thought to piranhas. They were abstract things, and existed in my imagination in turns as swarms of tiny ravenous sharp-toothed guppy-like things that would shred and dissolve a body in seconds, or as giant fish with open snapping mouths like rabid dogs and gums lined with razor-sharp prongs that would swallow a person whole. But here they were, foot-long creatures that humans fished for their meat, and whose bite a person could survive. When you held them up to the light, or rather, held this man's thumb up to the light, they didn't seem so scary after all.

The next morning, we packed up and said goodbye and the naturalist rode with us on the canoe for two hours, back to the bridge where we'd say goodbye. I was surprised by how sad I felt about leaving. He hugged me goodbye, and I climbed into the shuttle, and pressed the side of my forehead to the glass as we drove away past thick forest. Then, unexpectedly, I started to cry, and leaned further into the window so Anna and the others wouldn't see. I didn't know if it was our leaving the naturalist or the rainforest that I was crying over, maybe it was both, and the thought of going back to Los Angeles, where I'd lived for a decade, with its strip malls and its freeways, away from these trees and these birds and this quiet. Normal, I supposed. I knew I was not the first person to feel sad leaving a beautiful green place, and a new romance, to take a long bus ride back to reality, which had paused while we were disconnected in the jungle. Besides: what a lucky thing to be sad about.

In Quito that night, after an eight-hour bus ride back to the city, the naturalist and I texted briefly, and I was hopeful that it would continue. But a few days later his texts dwindled and then, silence.

III

Back in L.A. I'd been on a few dates with someone, and after I returned we tried to make plans, but we couldn't find a time to meet. First, he got sick. Then he went on a work trip. Then I got sick. And then he was going on another trip to see his family overseas, and didn't want to see me in case I made him sick again.

"I do really want to see you," he said.

"Me too," I said. But I didn't know if that was true. My heart wasn't in it.

The night before he left for his second trip, we did see each other. I wanted to try, to see if something could work with him. We had dinner, and then went back to his place. We had planned that I would sleep the night so we could spend as much time together as possible before he left. But sitting on his couch we had an argument. It was about something we'd been texting about on and off for a month or so, a dream he'd spun about a cabin he was going to build me in the woods someday with a custom-built library. It had been cute when we were first talking about it, but this hypothetical cabin started to feel off to me as more details and conditions materialized: it had to be isolated, he said, off-grid, a place we'd commit to living in full time, and also, I'd have to be on my best behavior for fifteen years if I was going to get the library. Well, the off-grid part sounded perfect, with the right person. But the part about behaving felt a bit too parental for comfort. What if I wanted a conditions-free library?

"Better be super rich then," he said.

Somehow the conversation spun out of control that night on the couch. I kept snagging on the word "behave," and he couldn't understand why it was bothersome to me. I was overreacting, he said.

"Maybe it's just my resistance to authority," I told him.

I said this with a joking smile, but in my heart I thought this: I really don't want to be with a man who tries to control me. I want an equal partnership, where it's okay if we mess up as long as there is honesty and trust and love and communication there. And laughter, and lightness. Little things he had said and was saying made me feel like, in time, he would become this subtle authority in my life, even though he insisted that wasn't what he wanted to be.

We couldn't find a resolution to the cabin conversation on the couch, and so we went to bed, tense energy between us. I felt unsettled. I told him I was tired and on the last day of my period and just wanted to sleep. This was all true. He was disappointed. I was wearing cute pajamas, a black silk romper-type thing with short shorts and spaghetti straps. They were all I had, but I soon wished I'd worn something else. In bed he kept putting his hands all over me, and I kept telling him no. Maybe I had been unclear the first time, I thought. So I said it again, louder this time.

"You're asking for it in those sexy little pajamas," he said.

I had no words for that, but thankfully afterwards there was only silence.

In the morning we had sex. I had relented because he'd somehow made me feel guilty about withholding my body from him, and also I'd convinced myself that maybe it would be okay. But it wasn't, because I wasn't. Afterwards, I felt a pit in my stomach. I left his place and in my heart I knew that it was over.

While he was away on his trip, I heard from the naturalist again. Within a few days we were texting a lot, and then texts all day turned into video calls every night. He was sweet, and he felt safe. I wondered if it was because he was so far away. When he was in the jungle he'd go silent, sending a text over wifi in the evenings to check in, and then we'd talk again on video call when he was back in Lago Agrio. He started calling me his girlfriend, as a joke. I started calling him my boyfriend. As a joke.

I wondered if I was running away from something real with the cabin guy and toward a fantasy life with someone who represented an escape from my life in L.A. This is what I'd been told: that I was always running from something. From people, from places. All those short relationships I'd had in L.A. with people who were emotionally unavailable or who were available but whom I'd somehow convinced myself were not right for me. Here was a potential relationship in the city I lived in, someone who was wanting a relationship, and though it was proving difficult before it had even reached velocity, maybe we could work through everything with some compromise. The cabin guy was a little stern, he was particular, he made me feel uneasy, but our lives matched up in a way that my life and the naturalist's life simply did not. We had things in common, many more than a simple love for the rainforest. Still, I couldn't seem to let him go, this gentle man lying in a hammock in the jungle texting me goodnight with a piranha scar thumb.

And so, when the cabin guy was back in town, we had our final conversation at the botanical gardens near my house, and sat, unplanned, at the top of a jungle walk, where I told him that I just didn't think we were compatible enough for things to move forward. I didn't tell him that there was another person, out there in the real jungle, that I was turning my heart toward instead. It was dishonest. But the part about us not being compatible was true, and it was already reason enough to end things before they really got started. It didn't feel right with him. He argued against it, and the conversation dragged on in circles until I couldn't bear it anymore and I told him he couldn't use reason to argue with my feelings and we said goodbye.

IV

A few months later I returned to Ecuador. The naturalist wanted to see me again, but he couldn't enter the United States, he said. There was a near one-year wait for a tourist visa, and he hadn't joined the waiting list yet because he wasn't confident they would approve him anyway. He couldn't yet demonstrate the sort of ties to his home country that the immigration authority would want to see: investments, property in his name, a family he'd be leaving behind. They'd see him as a risk for overstaying his visa. I knew how difficult the US immigration system was to navigate, because I'd gone through so many visas myself. So I offered to go back to his country.

We rented an apartment for ten days in Quito and walked around the city every afternoon, along cobblestone streets through the old town, the naturalist in guide mode, showing me the historic buildings, taking me to his favorite places to eat. He'd gone to a university in the city and so he knew it well.

"Make sure you drink a lot of water," he'd reminded me. "For the altitude."

Some mornings I had to work, and the naturalist went to the market to buy eggs and vegetables and fruit, and he'd prepare breakfast: scrambled eggs with peppers and onion and spinach, fresh juice. This was, he said, how he ate every day.

In the afternoons we stopped in cafes for Andean hot chocolate and sat in the sunshine on tiny balconies lined with geraniums, watching the world bustle by us below. We ate steaming chicken soup, humitas, or savory ground corn steamed in the husk, and llapingacho, a traditional dish with chorizo, potato patties, and egg. We drank hot chicha made with fermented manioc and jugs full of fresh juice made with granadilla or maracuya, two types of passion fruit. We took a taxi up the Panecillo, a loaf-shaped hill known as "the bread roll" with a 135-foot-tall aluminum statue of a winged Virgin Mary, guardian and mother of Quito, who gazed out over the city, one hand raised in benediction. In the early evening we ate in a restaurant just below her, high up on a balcony that looked out over the plateau of twinkling lights on the eastern slopes of Pichincha volcano, a city some 9,350 feet above sea level.

At night, the streets were empty.

"It never used to be like this," he said later that night when we were walking to a bar along a strip that used to be the center of the city's nightlife. "Ever since the issues with the cartels people are scared to go out now. Quito has changed."

On day four, we went out walking to find lunch and stopped in a small ceviche spot inside a hidden mall. We sat down to eat at a little plastic table, and the white fish in my ceviche seemed off but I didn't want to be impolite, so I ate some anyway. It really didn't smell good.

"How is it?" he asked me.

"Honestly, I don't know if it's good."

He held a spoonful of fish to his nose and flinched. "No," he said. "I don't think that's good to eat. Do you want something else?"

I told him I'd get something later and sat and picked at the onion while he finished his meal. This was a mistake. Whatever was in the fish had been soaking into the onion as well, but I didn't think about that, and then we left and I didn't think of the fish again.

Not until day five. I woke up with an unbearable pain in my stomach. The bathroom was right at the foot of the bed we were sleeping in, only a sliding door between where the naturalist slept and where I needed to rid myself of whatever was making me so ill. When he went to the kitchen at the other end of the house, I made my run for the toilet. The situation was bad. And loud.

"I need to stay in today," I told him later, curled up and sweating in the bed.

He had just come out of the shower, his long hair twisted up in a towel like he was at a hotel spa. "Por que?"

"I'm not feeling good," I said. "You should go out, though."

"No," he said, rubbing his hair in the towel. "I'll stay with you."

"I think I have food poisoning." My stomach rumbled again and I laughed, sweat tingling on my forehead. "Can you go away for a minute please? I need the bathroom and it's going to be loud."

"Don't worry about it," he said. "Son los sonidos de la selva."

The sounds of the jungle, he said.

All those years in the rainforest, in the garden, looking for pockets of nature in the city, and this was the first time in my life that I had been allowed to feel that my body was nature, too, and that I didn't need to shame it into silence.

That weekend we left our suitcases in the apartment in Quito and took a bus into the Amazon again, stopping outside of Lago Agrio where we stayed with his family, on their small farm at the edge of the rainforest where they grew corn and yucca, cacao and citrus, and where his mother kept over a hundred chickens.

"She loves her chickens," he told me. "They're like her pets."

"Do you eat them, too?"

"Yes." He laughed.

Street dogs that had shown up, been fed, and decided to stick around as guard dogs roamed the property, and one mother hen led a flock of tiny ducklings around the house that she had decided were her children, never mind the tiny bills instead of beaks. We sat in the open-air kitchen and ate his mother's chicken soup, made with a bird that had been sacrificed that morning, and a traditional dish called maito: tilapia fish wrapped in the sturdy leaf of a bigao plant and cooked over coals, served on the bright green leaf with steamed sticks of yucca and a small tomato and onion salad. Everything they ate, he told me, was grown or caught on the property, save for tomatoes, onions, and rice. Everything they ate was a regalito de la Pachamama. A little gift from Mother Earth.

We hiked into the rainforest at the back of their property with his mother and a handful of nieces and nephews, who climbed trees and swung from the vines along the way. The humid air was rich with the smell of wood and earth and leaves. We arrived at a clearing where his parents grew white cacao, and his mother sliced open a giant fruit with thick yellow and red skin. Inside were rows of seeds covered in sticky, translucent white pulp. The kids demonstrated how to suck the fruit off the seeds, which his parents would later dry and sell to be turned into chocolate. It was sweet seeing how the naturalist looked out for the kids, and how much they admired him.

That night in his small room, distant trucks roaring along the highway to and from the Colombian border, we lay under a mosquito net in the naturalist's bed while a gecko clicked from the ceiling.

"I know it's humble here," he said. "Probably different to what you are used to."

It was different to my life in L.A., yes, but I didn't know how to tell him how much like home it really felt there. I thought of the old house I'd grown up in in Australia, deep in rural apple country, the dirt on the floor and the lizards and mice inside, the forever-broken windows patched up with newspaper. I thought of running through the paddocks to the back of the property, past the fruit trees and the muddy ponds and the chickens, of snakes in the grass and of crunching through the forest in sandals. Thought of the easier times before that, of our house on the mountain, backed by rainforest where my brother and I would clamber over moss-covered trunks and swing from vines and dig our little hands into damp decay, then we'd run home and watch other kids on television and I'd dream of someday living in the city.

Here in the Amazon it felt like I'd stumbled upon a specific discomfort I'd been running away from ever since I was seventeen and moved out of home, that somehow I'd been moving in a circle this whole time, and had finally reached the 359th degree, had found some strange parallel universe to the one I had known. His life was different, I knew this. Me and my family were descendants of European settlers; his family's ancestors had suffered at the hands of the Spanish, and still fought today for the right to care for their ancestral lands and protect them from resource extraction that, farther north, I probably benefited from in some way. I moved freely throughout the world on my passport, while he had never traveled abroad, would not always be welcomed on the lands I set foot on so easily. We were each dependent on a different Amazon for our food, our materials, our income. Our lives were not the same. And yet despite all of that, in this little room with a singing gecko, at the edge of this hurting forest, there was some comfort in how familiar this place, and he, felt. I hoped someday I could show him the mountain I used to call home.

V

Three months after that trip, we are back in the jungle behind his parents' property. He wants to camp tonight, to escape the sounds of trucks that rattle along the road, to retreat into the serenity of the rainforest, where only the songs of the river and frogs and insects can keep us awake. And so, we hike along the track his parents have forged through the green, and we breathe the beautiful rot that steams from the forest floor.

It's hard to imagine that much of the rainforest around Lago Agrio has been destroyed; here it is alive and thrumming with the songs of crickets and monkeys, tanagers and his mother's chickens, who cluck from their pens at the edge of the forest. We get to the Rio Aguarico around sunset, and we set up our tent in a small clearing in the forest, then clamber down a muddy switchback to reach the river, its stones still warm from the day's sun. The naturalist drags a fallen tree to the pebbles and breaks up the wood to make a campfire. We cook packet ramen we bought from the supermarket in the city and watch lightning crack against purple sky on the horizon, though the sound of thunder never reaches us. When it is time to sleep we climb back up through the forest, all black now with very little moonlight filtering through the canopy, and I, a coward in the dark despite growing up in Australian rainforest and bush myself, zip us tight into the tent without wasting any time outside. When our conversation tapers off, we listen to the concert in the trees and understory outside. Things sound louder at night, the other senses dulled.

There are, I have read, three million species living in the Amazon, plant and animal, and individuals must number in the quintillions, those higher numbers that a human brain cannot and need not comprehend. All there is to know is that here, every inch pulses with life. The ground, a marvel in its composition of fallen leaves, is teeming with spiders, beetles, ants, and other beings that build their homes here, invisible to the eye of larger mammals. In the tallest trees, bromeliad plants hug trunks and lounge in the crevices of branches; up in the forest canopy they form entire micro-ecosystems, each a city of its own, some of the bowl-shaped plants holding several liters of water in tiny living pools, which render them a suitable home to a hundred or more species of insects, frogs, and other unseen residents. A tree felled is never just a tree felled, and if it is a tree with a hundred wax-leafed epiphytes pinned to its body, then it is a universe lost, communities displaced as their cities spill onto the duff.

"Many trees have been cleared here in the past," the naturalist explains, "so this is considered secondary forest."

He means forest that suffered some grave human disturbance but has since regenerated naturally, though it has yet to reach the end point of ecological succession, which is perhaps a point marked by thicker, louder, more vibrant soundscapes.

He explains that the area was covered in coffee plants twenty years ago. "Then when my parents got the land, they allowed it to regrow."

I think of the coffee grinds I had squirreled into our camping pack to prepare in the morning, and I wonder how many bromeliad cities, how many frog concert halls and insect opera houses were demolished in some other part of the rainforest for that small handful of beans that were crushed and will be, tomorrow morning, strained with scalding water into a camping cup. Perhaps when it was still primary forest the songs were louder, though it's hard to imagine.

In the middle of the night, I wake to a sharp pain in my back and a strange silence. When you are in the Amazon, a place that doesn't sleep, and you are meant to be surrounded by spiny devil katydids and tawny-bellied screech owls and all manner of creatures that work the night shift, you notice silence when it occurs, and when everyone is silent all at once it worries you. I shift on the sleeping mat, the hard ground pressing into my hip, and I wonder if a predator is outside, if that is why the song stopped. Or perhaps, finally, the forest fell asleep. Where are the screeches, the squeaks, the stridulations and stuttering trills? Where are the zits and the lisps and the tsip-tsip-tsips? Where are the barks and mews and croaks of frogs broadcasting their location to their damp-skinned communities?

"Where did you all go?" I whisper in my own silence to the tops of the trees, to the understory leaves, to the wet forest floor.

The forest does not answer. Perhaps, right now, we are alone. We are both sleeping inside a tent inside a quiet heart that is supposed to be beating but has gone still. The naturalist is breathing next to me; I can hear the rise and fall of his chest. But the silence outside is unnerving, and it sends me into my head, starts to make me question my own alone-ness.

Here is this person that I am growing to love, but there is still a distance between us, a border, not only a physical border, but an emotional one. It must always be like that, I think. We are not like those trees I read about in Utah, a grove of quaking aspen, connected by their root system as one single living organism. We are separate beings. Each of us alone. You can never truly be connected to someone. No matter how close you get you're still just two beings, walking through life next to each other.

No, wait, I tell my brain. Stop that. This is not true.

We *are* connected. All of us, this tent, this forest, this earth, the air, the water. We're all just one big living, breathing organism. I'm sure I read an article about this. I will look it up when I get service again and—stop, I think again. You are spinning out. Go to sleep.

But my mind won't turn off and I can't get comfortable. Maybe the reason is this: There is a third in the tent with us. Below my soft belly, beneath layers of skin and fat and tissue and nerves and muscle, a raspberry sized bundle of cells and promise is growing steadily, tucked away in a ram head of an organ inside my pelvis, inside which my body is creating another organ, just for the occasion. This berry is not asleep and she is not awake. She is just there, silent, waiting to be told what part to grow next.

VI

In the last week of my previous trip to Ecuador, the naturalist and I were back in our apartment in Quito, all stomachs settled, lying on the bed with two glasses of red wine. He'd lit some palo santo and tea lights the apartment's owner had left on the shelves around us. We were talking about kids, and whether we wanted any, and I'd told him how I wanted to be a mother, and that I'd even thought about doing it alone in L.A.

"Te gustaría tener un bebe conmigo?" he asked.

Would I like to have a baby with him? The question was so unexpected, so matter-of-fact that I think I spilled a bit of red wine out of the corner of my mouth. I wasn't sure if I'd misunderstood the Spanish, wasn't sure if he was testing my expectations of him, which would be mortifying, or if he was offering to have a baby with me, which would be wild.

"What do you mean?" I asked, rubbing my lip with my thumb.

"Do you want to have a baby with me?"

"You want to have a baby? Sorry, I don't understand."

"Yes," he said. "If you would like to."

Of all the decisions to properly think about, this was probably a big one. I was probably falling in love with him, and yet we still barely knew each other, and I knew that it would take years to properly get to know him. But I'd also seen too many cases of people taking years to know somebody only to realize they made a mistake too far down the road, too long after the big decisions had been made. As one of my equally reckless friends would say: make the irreversible decision now, and you'll be forced to figure out how to make it work later. Go with what your gut tells you.

My gut—otherwise silent in that moment, thankfully—told me yes. Be wild.

"Yes, then." I smiled. "Let's have a baby together."

"But I would want to be in their life," he said. "Not just like a souvenir for you."

"No, of course." We both laughed at the absurdity of the situation.

"How would we make it work, not living in the same country?" I asked.

"I could visit," he said. "We could go on long trips. Ya sabes que quiero viajar."

That is true, I thought. I knew he wanted to travel.

"But could you ever live somewhere outside of the Amazon?"

I didn't know how someone so connected to the jungle could ever live far away from it. There was no rainforest in Los Angeles. But I didn't think I'd live in that city forever, either. Australia had rainforest. Maybe we could split our time between our two home countries.

"I could live anywhere," he said. "As long as there is nature, and you."

We were both red-wine optimistic about what it could look like. Perhaps it is a conversation that we will never stop having.

VI

It's not silent in the forest anymore. In the warm light of morning there is music again, oropendola songs ring like raindrops and squirrel monkeys twitter and peep in the treetops, as sunlight filters through leaves to warm the patch of damp earth where now the naturalist cracks twigs and tries to light another campfire a few meters from our tent. He is trying to light a campfire with wet sticks so we can boil eggs that somehow survived the hike in, and some water for my one daily allowed cup of coffee. Maybe, I think, now would be a good time to quit.

"How did you sleep?" he asks when I step out of the tent.

"Possibly the worst night's sleep of my life."

Now that I am pregnant, everything is uncomfortable, and I consider that a hike-in camping trip in the Amazon was maybe not the best idea. I'd done enough research on the area and had prepared enough appropriate clothing to not be worried about mosquito-borne troubles, but I already fell into a creek on his parents' farm yesterday when a log bridge snapped under my feet, and now my tailbone hurts and I am worried that falling into a creek in the Amazon when a log snaps under your feet is not something the pregnancy books will cover.

But sitting here in this small cathedral, the forest alive around us, the despair of last night starts to dissolve into the morning song. And I wonder, how could this place, so full of life, ever be quiet?

"Do you think the forest is ever silent?" I ask the naturalist.

He looks confused. "Here, silent?"

"I don't mean no truck noises. I mean totally silent. Last night there was this moment, around three a.m., when it seemed like there was no sound at all."

"I don't think so," he says, using a stick to turn the eggs, which vibrate in a pan of boiling water on the fire. "There are always night creatures."

Later I will read about how scientists measure the life of a rainforest by the quality of its sounds, and soundscapes in the Amazon can divine changes in population sizes and behavioral patterns in birds, frogs, insects, and many mammals—helping scientists understand how they are responding to changing conditions brought on by climate change. I will learn that researchers have described a "silent forest" as indicative of the presence of yellow fever having killed all the howler monkeys. I will learn that 16,000 minutes of acoustic monitoring in another part of the Amazon have told the scientists, the listeners, that a rainforest never sleeps. There is always music, in every minute of every day.

And I will wonder if maybe when I'd thought the forest was silent, it wasn't. Maybe the silence was all in my head. Or maybe, as we often do, I had bent my ear so far inward to hear my own thoughts that I had forgotten to listen to what was outside.

Confessions of a Free Woman

Carla Vianna

We have this idea of what a Free Woman should look like—
she has long, tangled hair,
almost always blowing in the wind.

she smiles with all 32 of her teeth,
her happiness cause for envy.

she dances with her eyes closed,
because she doesn't care who's watching.

she blends into the ocean, the sunset, the forest—
her nature transcends the physical world.

    she is the changing tides,
    the orange glow in the sky,
    the roots beneath the trees.

I've traveled far to find this Woman,
because, of course, a Free Woman belongs to no single place or person.
I've been told that a Free Woman roams,
so,
I'm roaming.

I am alone,
wandering a small town in rural Mexico,
with no one to tell me where to go,
what to do,
or who to be.

a tiny flat in a local family's yard,
my very own stained glass window,
small piles of ash on the terracotta tiles,
from my incense sticks and cigarettes,

I light another,
lying there topless, in flowered underwear,
put on my favorite song,
and smoke out my chapel.

I've stitched together the perfect image of a Free Woman—
yet when I snoozed my alarm clock today,
I felt a familiar sting of guilt.

It's a Tuesday, and I slept in.

I woke up in this big bed by myself,
and I felt bad about that, too.

I sort of wished you were here.

I ordered carbs for breakfast for the fifth day in a row,
and I felt really bad about that.

I haven't worked out in weeks.

For a moment, I even missed my routine back home,
and I felt especially terrible about that.

Routines are for the trapped.

And then it hits me:
freedom isn't something I can map out on a Pinterest board,
or build out of boarding passes to far-off destinations.
Believe me, I've tried.

A Woman's Freedom comes from within.
If you dug into the core of every Free Woman,
you wouldn't find a list of rules or expectations—
only unconditional acceptance.

True freedom is accepting that I snoozed the alarm clock
and woke up alone,
and indulged in the carbs,
and wished you were here,
and missed my routine,
despite my desperate attempt to live up to this fixed idea of what a
Free Woman should be.

The freedom I want comes from honoring my true nature—
from allowing myself to be the brave,
scared,
broken,
strong,
lost,
and confident woman I am—
both at home and thousands of miles away.

Paperbacks

Courtney Hanks

She says to him—

    Grandpa died just before I turned fifteen, and the following summer, Mom sent me to Connecticut to help Grandma pack up the trailer. It was by a lake where they spent their summers, and I had spent a week every summer since I was five, a place where the sun blazed hot during the day, and the nights had a chill I only knew in winter in Georgia. You know a place like it, I'm sure. I think we all do.

    Those summer visits were the only time I saw my mom's parents, with them living so far away. So they were always strangers. And they always weren't.

    That lakeside trailer used to be all barefoot Connecticut summers catching fireflies in glass jars, lying in the shade under blueberry bushes and bursting into their bitter flesh with my tongue, and riding with Grandpa on the boat after he let me drive. Grandpa would take me fishing, teach me how to hold a rod, how to reel it in, the way to hook a worm. I kept a straight face in the shadow of his instruction while the worms danced, dying beneath my fingers. I hated sitting still, being quiet, but I was a good girl for him. We'd return after hours in the sun and show off our catch to Grandma, who always acted more excited than she felt.

    Grandma spent most of her days cooking or crocheting blankets and dish rags. She even crocheted a set of red and white checkered lawn chairs. I have one of them now, on my back porch, that I got after she died last year.

With Grandpa gone and me being fifteen, the summer felt like a dead thing. Mom didn't come with me, and I was pissed at her for it. It was the biggest fight we'd had, and no matter how much I complained, begged, and pleaded with her, she wouldn't let me stay home. I didn't talk to her for days after arriving, not until the night of the fire.

The lake looked and sounded the same. But the trees building the surrounding forest pointed up, up, and up, like they were telling me to look away, and their leaves turned early; green tipped orange in July, a change that came too soon. And Grandma was still Grandma, just worse.

Grandma believed supper should be served at five thirty, and you said your prayers before eating. She believed little girls should say please and thank you and ask to be excused from the table, that every woman should know how to cook a decent pie, and that slutty was the worst thing for a girl to be. She would have me roll her sparse, short hair in foam curlers and paint her nails pink. With Grandpa gone and me not being a little girl anymore, I didn't know what to be with her, who to be, and I generally avoided her sour look of disappointment she'd give me when I slipped up.

The trailer was too much for Grandma to keep up with, and Mom said she'd need the money from selling it. It was my job to help her pack everything and clean up before I left, and since I'd arrived, Grandma had refused to pack a single box.

While she slept, I'd pass the night hours in a sort of bored and painful insomnia, until the night I found a box of romance novels hiding in a cabinet. In those late, aching hours shuffling through hidden nooks and crannies along the floor and seat benches of the trailer, under a wad of mismatched yarn, I found them. We're talking hot, descriptive romance novels, sex scenes and all. I didn't tell her I found them. I couldn't imagine my thin-lipped grandmother, who once left a party because someone pointed out that "my boobs were coming in," reading books with lines like, "She touched his velvet rod of soft steel," and "He reached into the wetness building at the apex of her thighs."

I'd smuggle them out of the trailer in a tote bag, hiding under blueberry bushes to read with my pulse surging and belly warming. Breasts heaved and teeth tugged at sensitive flesh, and couples moaned breathlessly between pages. Tension flitted between my legs, and I imagined some faceless man pulling at my buttons; my wanting opened its eye.

Up until this point, my experience with boys had been mostly making out at parties I'd lied to my mom about, and that one time a boyfriend of mine surprised me by slipping his hand down my jeans, a startling sweep of his thick fingers.

At fifteen, I felt men's eyes when I read alone in my room, when I took a shower, when I ate an ice cream cone or a hot dog; I felt them on me like a comb through hair, trying to snag on some part.

When I dressed, it was like a boy sat watching from the edge of my bed. At school, I'd see them in their swarms in the hallways, imagine their eyes. I'd fall in love a little bit with a boy I'd never talked to and paint them into whole narratives; he loved the way I tucked my hair behind my ear when I felt anxious—or else he'd love my laugh, how it sounded like music or angels singing. I don't know if you ever felt like that, or if all girls felt this way, but I did.

I showed off my skin in any way I could. I'd seen my mom tug at her body, pulling it into jeans or hiding it under loose shirts. She'd mumble about her age, stretch marks, or a new vein. I knew I was supposed to pick my body apart, but I didn't. It felt like power.

That summer, it was still all new to me, and I performed for it. When I left the trailer in my cut-off shorts, I'd remove my T-shirt and hide it in my tote bag, instead wearing a cherry red string bikini top. I'd slick black liner on my lids, pump on mascara. In the forest of trees, in the barren, grassy fields, and on the empty dirt road, I felt men's eyes on me, nodding: yes, yes, yes.

I shaved my legs every day.

Anyway, there was this guy Jimmy down at the convenience store most afternoons. He would go out fishing early and then come back, wash off his gear, and go home to his trailer a few rows down from Grandma.

As far as crushes go, my little love stories, I gave him a big one. He made it worth my time, too, giving me as good of an object as any to form my fantasy around. He wore these old, stretched tanks that draped off his shoulders, revealing golden skin like fall leaves, and it shined, glistening with sweat and sunscreen oil, firm. He had a man's body, more like the men on television or in my paperbacks. He had a quick way of moving, the way some dogs can be, sort of jumping into each movement with a jolt. But his mannequin smile always slammed into me hardest.

When I'd get a Coke or a popsicle from the old clerk inside the store, I'd imagine his eyes following me through the glass, and when I chatted with him outside, I took his smile like a gift, something given carefully. I didn't need any of it to be real.

It became a sort of routine.

Grandma would kick me out of the trailer. I don't know what she did all day. She said she was packing, but the most I'd seen her do was lift objects, something like a clock or a pillowcase, stare at it for ten minutes, then put it back into the same spot.

Outside, I read books in the grass or under the blueberry bushes until the sun turned, and then I'd walk to the convenience store in my bikini top. Jimmy would tell me stories, mostly about fishing, but also about his time competing in professional water skiing. He'd done really well, too, and could have gone to the Olympics. Everyone said it. A bad accident blew out his right knee, and his dream drowned in that black lake water. I'd listen to him talk for an hour, wondering if he could smell my cherry lip gloss, imagining his hands on my waist, his clever, long fingers pulling at me like I'd seen him handle a rope. The books gave me a whole new vocabulary for what I wanted.

I knew I should be helping Grandma, making her build boxes, sorting through the junk in the trailer, and getting myself back home. I felt restless though; anger tangled against my tongue, bitter, and it built up into my chest threatening to come out in a scream, and so I hid it in my stories, buried it on the lake's beach with all the things I didn't feel like belonged to me anymore. They don't tell you that part about growing up, about how the fireflies and barefoot dancing, the singing at the top of your lungs and drawing ugly pictures don't feel like they are yours anymore. How the world becomes something different because you are different, and you didn't mean for it to happen, and you didn't know it was happening in the first place.

I felt loneliest at night with Grandma.

We'd eat supper. I am sure we must have talked, but I don't remember saying a word or hearing it outside of the Lord's Prayer. I'd clean up all the dishes while she played solitaire on her laptop, and then we would sit on the porch to watch the sunset and eat ice cream, her hands busy with cheap yarn and her crochet hooks. She'd tried to teach me a few years back. I never got the hang of it. You know how I get when something isn't immediately easy for me.

When seven hit, she would say goodnight, closing the accordion door to her room, and I wouldn't see her again until morning. I'd spy in her things. Aside from the paperbacks, there were heavy albums filled with photos from Grandma and Grandpa's life together. Mom must have had thirty cousins, while I only have the two in California. I wondered what it would have been like to be raised in a big family, to have parents and siblings, and more cousins that I could name all living within a few towns of each other.

Grandma and Grandpa's black-and-white wedding photograph hung at the front of the trailer in an oval frame. In the photo, my grandfather stood there, handsome in his white naval uniform. It looked a lot like that photo your mom has in the kitchen, by the sink.

I could hardly see my grandma in the girl she was. Grandpa called Grandma his sweetheart, kissing her even when they were old, and I hoped to fall in love like that.

This is a conversation I do remember. Grandma caught me staring at the photo one night and asked if she looked pretty. It wasn't that she wasn't pretty in her white hat and short veil, dark hair curled under her ears; she was. But there was always something ugly about her, something in the cut of her lips, like a frown lived in the hidden corner of her smile, a vacant tug of unhappiness. But I didn't say that.

I said yes; she looked pretty.

She told me she was nearly eighteen when she got married. Neither she nor Grandpa finished high school, and he enlisted a year before. I remember thinking she was only two years older than I was, then, when she married him.

She said she'd never lived on her own. She'd lived with her parents and then Grandpa.

I asked when we would start packing up.

The following day I saw Jimmy, and it was like he was waiting for me. His fishing gear piled, all washed and stacked in his truck.

He said he thought he'd missed me today, or maybe I had left. When I said I was stuck here until Grandma finished packing the trailer, he asked why it was taking so long. It was then I felt that attention, his attention, that he remembered a detail of mine. Had tucked it away somewhere.

I was really missing Mama, the feel of her fingers through my hair, the smell of her white floral perfume.

He nodded and asked what kind of things I liked, suddenly interested, his attention heavy and close. He smelled like fish and sunscreen, and the musk of something sour. I tried to think of grown-up woman things to say, deciding on cooking, seeing as how all the women I knew cooked, with my grandma's pies and my mother's casseroles. I let out a breath when he just nodded. We were standing close to each other by the truck, and when I squinted up against the sun, he leaned over me to shade my eyes.

And then the picture formed.

I wasn't there by the truck; I was several steps back, seeing myself as though I was in a photograph, the shrinking space between our bodies, his presence looming, the shadow he created darkening so that my details disappeared in the picture. I liked how it looked on the outside, golden and happy. Now that reality towered before me, I couldn't reel myself in, couldn't feel the visible happiness of the photograph version. He smiled as his head lowered to mine, his teeth bone white, and brushed his paper lips against my cheek. He told me I was pretty.

There was no rush of warmth, no electric tension building under my skin. My head emptied aside from Grandma and the way she looked at herself in that wedding photo. The twisted thing in my stomach blistered, and I backed up. I don't know what I said before leaving, if I said anything at all.

Half conscious, I walked back to the trailer with a roar like the wind in my head, in my chest, like a wailing cry. I'd tripped on a realization, and now that it was here, I didn't have a place for it.

Grandma stood outside the trailer in her pink muumuu. She stared up through smoke, I recognized, from one of Grandpa's old cigarettes. I'd never seen her smoke before, and the smell of it brought me back to an out-of-reach time. In the lines on her face, in the angle of her eyes, I felt a turn in her in the way that a decision made can change everything about you, even the way you look. I hadn't replaced my shirt, and she saw me there in my red bikini top, black makeup painted on my eyes, a kind of heartbreak shaking through me, and looked at me as cold-eyed as gunmetal. I came beside her to stare up at the trailer, the same height now, I realized. We watched the nothing together in silence. When she took my hand in hers, it felt like the most natural thing in the world, and I noticed I had been crying, though I didn't know what for. We must have stood like that for an hour. Then, she talked.

She told me about Grandpa, and how when they were younger, he would get mean after too much drinking and tell her she was fat. How he knew that would hurt her. She told me how hard it was when he went on long hunting trips, leaving her alone with three girls by herself. She wasn't sure she should have been a mother, but she was so young when she got married that she didn't know much of anything about herself. Didn't know how to ask. She said she loved to cook, or that she used to. No better feeling. For that hour, she just talked, like she'd been gnawing on her whole life since the day Grandpa passed, the animal it was, and was afraid of stopping and choking on it all.

She ended it by saying, I won't pack it up.

I knew she meant the trailer. And so I asked her, what do you want to do then? And she met my eye, and without a flicker of rage or anything, said, burn it down.

And that's what we did. I had my first glass of wine at fifteen while sitting in one of her green lawn chairs, just watching it all go: the photo albums, the wedding photo, the pots and pans, the yarn, the romance novels, everything.

The smoke would turn, and we'd have to move our chairs, and people spoke to us, asking questions probably, but we were in a bubble of something. She smiled at me, that ugly thing tugging at the very edge, and I thought, we must have that same smile.

Sneaking Around

Erin DiCamillo

As a teenage girl, I would, on occasion,
sneak into the boy next door's basement
in the hours after our parents fell asleep—or so we believed.
To watch TV, but mostly to kiss each other.
Pretty innocent stuff, really.
We were Catholic.
At my baby shower, each woman took turns
sharing her motherly wisdom and the boy next door's mother said,
    "Never say my kid would never . . .
      because one day you'll be falling asleep
      and hear the voice of the girl next door in your basement."
She had tucked away that story for twenty good years,
longed to laugh about it with the good girl who snuck around with her
    good boy.
We were the kind of kids who would never . . .

But it's occurred to me—not in that moment of my baby shower—
but in the years after, after experiencing the wisdom the women laid
    upon me,
that a lot of Motherhood—*girlhood, womanhood*—
is about sneaking around.

I used to sneak into our pantry for cookies when my mother's back was
    turned.
Sometimes still my husband catches me sneaking a bite of something
    sweet
and reminds me it is okay, is safe, to eat.

I used to tuck away tampons underneath my groceries,
if that's what you call frozen pizzas and pints of Ben & Jerry's.
Pay the cashier with averted eyes,
as if the tampons were the naughty thing I'd sneak inside my body
    later that day.

Sneak around to Planned Parenthood, too,
for my first birth control prescription because I hadn't learned
how to navigate the medical system yet and it seemed
like that's what you do if you're trying to sneak away your sins.
Like the girls who used to be (still are)
snuck away to a distant relative's home in another state,
only to return nine months later.

And then, there was work.
Work, work, work. So much work.
And the sneaking away of my spirit too,
under some storied illusion of success and sometimes insanity.

I started to rediscover her, my Spirit, when
I would sneak around to the gym to exercise, to
rediscover the strong, stretchy limbs I once had.

Strengthened them enough to walk away from one role
to another, and then to another—the call of Motherhood
stronger than any other.

And with this call came sneaking around to doctor's appointments,
blood draws, acupuncture, ultrasounds, minor surgeries even.
To keep showing up all the while sneaking away
this little, BIG thing emerging inside of me.

Sneaking away extra snacks and bathroom breaks,
the smell of vomit, deep sighs of overwhelming fear,
grimaces that betrayed a cool, collected front.
The fact that this baby—my son—even existed inside of me,
a secret I snuck away until 12 weeks or so
when his existence finally felt safe enough to share.

I felt a deep desire to talk about him constantly,
about everything I was experiencing.
And when labor came and went,
I wanted a stage upon which to share my story,
a story I share with my husband, nurse, and doctor,
a story few others have asked me to share.
That story of when the doctor walked in on my primal striptease,
hands grabbing the pole over the toilet seat,
gyrating my wide, child-bearing hips.
Over my wolfish howls, faintly hearing him say,
"I've never seen it done like that before."

There, I said it.
Many a woman has done it and none like any other.
And it feels damn powerful to share it.

And it felt powerful to feed my child,
even if I felt like I had to sneak away my breasts to do it.

And it felt powerful to meet with other women
and realize our wrecked human bodies could somehow summon
more, more, more for our babies.

It feels powerful that my child can take me to the
depth of wounds I didn't even realize I had snuck away
and keep on living anyway.

And it feels powerful to write this poem,
share it upon a stage,
and sneak around no more.

Woman of the House

Julia Burke

I adorned the walls
of my apartment
hanging decor myself
took my blazer off after work,
hung it on the shelf
I open tricky jars
check if I hear a bad guy at night
put on my nastiest face
ready to full-on fight
I look right in strangers' eyes,
walking from my car at night,
they can come at me
if they want, but it won't be
an easy fight
I tuck myself in
with warm tea and soup when sick
bought myself flowers
at the market
just because, I did
I bring all the groceries
inside in just one trip
I'm a regular at the gym

where I effortlessly run two miles,
then lift
I pay my bills ahead of time
all my money from the very first dime
I've worked for—
it's mine
I've taken care of myself by
myself;
I've created this beautiful life.

Postcards from New Hampshire

Anneke Bender

Dried vomit cakes the wheelchair spokes and has pooled along the rim, a clump that spins in a circle as I push Mr. Comstat to the patio. I am vaguely anxious that the clump will drop and get crushed under the wheel, but whatever. The floor hasn't been cleaned in the month I've been working at Elm Garden Nursing Home, and we are currently rolling over the remnants of worse things. The brain has an astonishing ability to lower expectations, like when new parents slide diarrhea into a garbage can with their bare hand.

One of my girlfriends actually did that, and called to tell me, worried about what her life had become. I'm not sure why she called me because I've never had kids, but maybe it was life chaos in general that was the commiserating feature. As luck would have it, I've never shit myself, but she's seen me slurring, fall-down drunk enough times to know I do not have my life under good control. Did not. Do now. *God grant me the serenity.*

It was my propensity for consuming too much alcohol that drove me to take this temporary nursing gig in a small New Hampshire town, and to live, temporarily, in a drafty farmhouse in the middle of winter. I am running away from Boston city life. *It's all temporary*, I keep telling myself. The problem is I can't see the future. I am 50 years old, hitting menopause (and other realities) like a brick wall, and have no idea where I go from here; because of this, my current circumstances have a way of feeling permanent.

It could be worse, of course, and this a balm I apply to all manner of wounds. Christina, the night nurse, once overdosed during her shift and the patients had to call 911; roused by Narcan, she was back at work the next week.

"You can't make this shit up," Don says.

Don is the nurse manager, a tall man with cropped hair who likely used to be in military-grade shape until the tribulations of age caught up with him. This is something we bond about, stumbling into a strange exchange after I try to explain our rising scale numbers by noting that muscle is heavier than fat.

"A pound of muscle equals a pound of fat," he says, shaking his head the same way my dad used to when he found my ideas absurd.

"Well, a pound of anything equals a pound of anything else, but equivalent volumes of, say, a bunch of feathers and a . . . bunch . . . of lead . . ." I start, but the sentence peters out.

Don continues to shake his head and laugh, wondering aloud what other nonsense they teach in the big city.

You really can't make this shit it up.

It seems to be the nature of the game in healthcare—at least in travel nursing—that you hit the ground running with no training whatsoever. And why would they train you? What does it behoove them to invest in a person who will be leaving in three or six months? You are just there to fill a seat, to accumulate charges for—in this case—Generation Healthcare, a multibillion-dollar company. I learn about its large coffers during a random Google search on my lunch break one day, turkey sandwich in hand; my jaw drops and a bit of turkey falls on the keyboard. I'm not sure why it surprises me. So much money fuels the healthcare industry these days that it can feel like 1980s Wall Street. *Greed is good. Greed works.* Scrolling through the publicly listed salaries, I learn that last year the CEO received a total compensation of $900,016 in base salary, $1,037,012 in incentive compensation, $650,000 for COVID-19 service, and $3,094,532 for something called "retention advance offsetting severance claims." I momentarily wonder about switching careers before a call light goes off, startling me from burgeoning fantasies of paid-off mortgages and student loans.

I have to learn what I can from my coworkers on the fly, in stolen moments. Every subset of healthcare has its own lexicon, and I am learning to speak SNF, or skilled nursing facility. Patients are steered in one direction or another based on what insurance will pay for—you have your Med A's and your Med B's, your "manageds." A NOMNC (Notice of Medicare Non-Coverage, pronounced *nom-nic*, the sound a Muppet might make while eating a cookie) means a patient will soon be getting kicked to the curb. An SNF is a transitional space between hospitalization and returning home, except that some people get stuck here, moving to the "other side" for long-term care.

"Can you do a hospice screen tomorrow?" Don asks me.

"Do you mean decide if a person is dying?" I ask, and then remark, for the record, that it seems like a doctor should make that call.

"Well, just assess if the dying might happen in the next three months or so."

I have to check my impulse to people please—it often takes more energy to explain why you don't feel comfortable doing something than it does to just quietly suppress your poorly defined ethical code. Logically, this is what Don is counting on. He seems most concerned with getting the things on his list done; I am a thing on his list and so is the patient who may or may not be dying.

In frustration, I wander into the hallway, feeling like I've missed the meeting where all necessary information was handed out, perhaps on a pamphlet with bullet points, text wrapping a picture of a smiling doctor looking at an elderly woman who is likewise smiling. Having missed the lesson, I feel as disoriented as the patients who inhabit Elm Garden's cramped rooms. I pass through the dining area where fifty old souls gather around a cheap piano and flat-screen TV and find myself wanting to sit down in a wheelchair alongside them.

Most days I share my shift with an older nurse named Mariam. Everyone calls her Mim, a non-ironic stand-in for *Mom*. She has old-school hair—short and fuzzy, fashioned into small curls and held in place by copious amounts of hair spray. Even her scrubs seem carefully tended, patterned with hearts or little bears.

"Every day, I try to leave the world a little better than how I found it," she is fond of saying, with a sweet smile. I am a sarcastic and cynical city-dweller—highly distrustful of kindness—but she really is genuinely sweet.

Mim works down one hallway and I work the other; we meet at the medication cart in the middle to trade stories about our patients and lives. Mr. Comstat is actually Mim's father, a dour man who has dementia and always feels like he is late for a meeting with his accountant. When he yells out, "What the fuck are you trying to sell me!" repeatedly, Mim is the only one who can calm him down. She goes into his room and whispers quietly in that sweet way of hers. Before you know it, he looks at least a little more resigned to his fate, leaving his roommate Larry—a former logger with a thick Bostonian accent—to breathe a sigh of relief.

I'm not sure if this is true, but it does seem like Mim's hallway is always a little . . . quieter? Than mine? She has a way, and not just with the patients. On Tuesday, Mim catches me in the middle of a wicked hot flash in the staff room, frantically fanning myself with copier paper and trying to suppress the urge to tear my shirt off; she doesn't say a word, just sits down next to me. As my fanning slows, the red blotches on my cheeks starting to fade, she looks at me with a smile.

"It's a bitch, innit?" she says.

The next day I find a small, battery-powered fan tucked in my locker.

Don tells me today that my patient Tom is moving to the other side. He needs a hip replacement, but before he can get his hip replaced, he needs to see a doctor to clear up a kidney infection, except the SNF won't pay to have him transported to the doctor, so he's stuck here.

Don is confusing me more and more. We spin around in circles and I say, "I don't know what that means." For instance, he tells me that in England socialized medicine pays for elective plastic surgery, but lets babies die.

"People are getting too many handouts," he says.

As far as I can tell, Elm Garden Nursing is not giving many handouts. They do not like to pay for much of anything, like janitorial staff, printer toner, and food. The cooks have a $5 per person, per day food allowance and it shows: canned carrots more yellow than orange, processed food in various shades of beige (mashed potatoes, chicken medleys, brown broccoli). Without a word—just looking at it—Larry and I laugh a good, hearty belly laugh one day, interrupted by the sound of Mr. Comstat throwing his tray against the wall.

"Tom should have checked with his insurance to see if they would pay for transportation to the doctor before he ever came here," Don says, barely looking up from the expense reports that are unreadable because the left side of each page is covered in a dark streak of ink.

"That's a terribly specific question to anticipate," I counter.

It's like Tom has been sucked into a healthcare vortex from which there is no escape, and he is in danger of lying in bed, racking up revenue for Generation Healthcare for the rest of his life.

I've been doing a lot of thinking about aging lately. It isn't hidden: we are all living a daily sacrifice to time. In my first month, we have already lost two patients—in the evening or on the weekend when things are quiet, they just go. And it feels like the daily confusions of dementia lie on a continuum I am already sliding down, my mind a spinning wheel as it tries to load the necessary word for—oh, I don't know—pencil. "Hand me that . . . thing . . . that . . . scribbles," I stutter, an object I need so I can write a reminder to myself about something I already forgot.

The years of winding up a life are also louder than I realized. One day while I am cleaning his room, Larry grabs my arm and yells, "Don't get trapped here." He has a grip so tight and holds on so long that I drop the spray bottle in my hand. "You still have your life," he shouts directly into my ear, not noticing the pool of cleaning fluid spreading across his floor, the toxic lemon smell filling the air.

It's strange how lucid people with dementia can sometimes seem, even when they're talking about the craziest things. Lorna—a woman who has managed through sheer grit and spitfire to make it to 97—sometimes tells me she better not see me around anymore because she knows I'm poisoning the food. The vitriolic rage behind her eyes is truly admirable. And Mim's father has become progressively convinced that he has been kidnapped—that he is really a very important person who belongs somewhere altogether nicer than Elm Garden Nursing Home. I want to tell him we are all too important to belong here, but there it is, and here we are.

Sometimes Mim and I take him to the patio so he can sit and talk, free to use the four-letter words that so irritate other staff. With the sun shining on our faces and Mr. Comstat cursing the plastic garden gnomes, all seems right with the world.

Around the patio, someone has placed birdfeeders every five feet or so, a situation that results in an ongoing turf war among the various feathered breeds: blue jays screech, robins bank on safety in numbers, hummingbirds zip about with a "catch me if you can" flair.

"It's like a sanctuary for difficult birds," Mim says one day.

"And difficult people," I add, as Mr. Comstat almost succeeds in kicking a squirrel.

Walking back inside, Mim looks me straight in the eyes and asks if I feel like my life has meaning and purpose. The question sets off a flurry of responses in my head, including questioning what about me would suggest I am without purpose and a general fear that we might soon start talking about Jesus. But then I strangely calm.

"I guess I'm trying to work that out," I say.

And I keep talking. I tell Mim that I don't know how to make decisions from anything other than vague notions. I've seen a lot of the world, but as an observer and not a participant. With tears in my eyes, I admit I am—pretty much utterly—lost.

She reaches out and rests her hand on mine the same way she does with her father. "You're doing so much better than you think you are," she says, winking at me. As the tears roll down my face, I really do almost believe her.

"What *happened?*" Laura, the head of cleaning, asks me, holding the remnants of a broken spray bottle in her hand. The low, edgy tone of voice makes her sound like a gritty detective out to solve a murder.

"I just dropped it?" I answer.

"Well, we're out of bottles and over budget for the year."

I can think of no response, and we stare at each other for several seconds. I finally blurt out, "For fuck's sake, I'll buy a bottle."

Later, I go to apologize for my outburst, weaving through a maze of hallways behind the kitchen stained with oil and old food. "Where is the cleaning department?" I keep asking, and people point in indistinct directions. I finally find her sitting in an office without windows, the broken spray bottle still on her desk. I tell her I wasn't frustrated with her, but with a company that won't buy bottles for cleaning fluid, not mentioning I just learned the CEO got paid $650,000 last year for "COVID-19 service," suddenly curious what that even means.

Driving home, my mood is as low as the sky, which is spitting out a strange rain-snow precipitation my windshield wipers toss aside in a gloomy rhythm. Rain is not very common in winter in New Hampshire.

"We're actually in a global cooling trend if you go back to when the world was first formed by volcanos," Don said this morning.

For some reason, the urge to drink is so strong that I start driving toward Rabbit Hollow Tavern, an impossibly cozy dive in a

1700s building *with a fireplace* and—most of the time—live local music that seems straight out of the Irish Midlands my family harkens from. A great place to drink. If I still drank. Which I don't.

On Monday, everyone is in a flurry because the state announced it will be coming for a site visit next week. Elm Garden's facility manager— George, a man who wears khakis with a crisply pressed white shirt *every day* and is typically only seen through the glass window of his office—starts combing through the facility for signs of noncompliance. He explains to us the importance of putting a date on our nursing communication forms and being able to identify where the defibrillators are. George is described by almost everyone as "on the spectrum" and typically only communicates via intercom. His voice is like Hal in *2001: A Space Odyssey*—a disembodied monotone that is the articulation point between the corporate office and the service workers who carry out what looks like care of elderly people, but is really just another way to make a lot of money.

George seems constantly underfoot as he walks around, looking behind doors for fire code violations, opening charts to ensure care plans are properly documented. He has an astonishing ability to ignore the constant blare of alarms, each of which indicates a patient need we address in a crazed, frenzied game of Whac-A-Mole. Running to get a new box of gloves so I can change Larry, who has soiled himself, George corners me in the hallway and starts telling me about a band he likes. *Uh-huh, uh-huh,* I say, reminding myself that he is on the spectrum, until, with dawning horror, I realize he's about to ask me on a date. We are mercifully interrupted by Mr. Comstat yelling, "Get me the fuck away from this smell or I'm going to kill Larry," and I spend the rest of the day diving into patient rooms when I see George coming.

As luck would have it, all hands are on deck the day of the site visit and the shift goes swimmingly well. Someone came to clean— apparently in the middle of the night—and the floors look shiny and new; I have 8 patients instead of the usual 20. Despite this, everyone seems to think that Elm Garden Nursing Home is in danger of being shut down. At the end of the day, when George's AI voice hums through the intercom asking everyone to come to the front of the building, we all look at each other and it independently passes through our minds that this is it: Elm Garden is closing.

Don signs back in from his lunch break so he can at least be paid for hearing the announcement. George exits his office with a big smile to greet the gathering crowd.

"We're going to show them how well things are going down here," he says, pointing to a cake.

At first I'm confused. Show who?

It turns out that the cake was sent to us in gratitude by the family of a resident who recently passed away, and George wants us all to take a picture to send to corporate. He precariously tilts the cake to make sure the top—*Thank you, Elm Garden* in swirling cursive blue icing—is visible. As more employees arrive, he just keeps staring forward, and I think someone should probably tell them they aren't being fired. Pictures are snapped from multiple phones as we say our requisite smiling words (*Elm Garden! Nurses Rule!* Inexplicably, *Brownies!*).

"This is why we do what we do. It's for the patients," George says.

For some reason, I have taken to scrolling through articles about the highest-paid executives in Generation Healthcare on my lunch break, and it is during one of these voyeuristic fits that I first see the picture. *The Generations of Generation Healthcare*. The CEO and his . . . *grandfather* . . . the former CEO.

No.

What?

My mind jumps and spins, lands upside down, then settles into a weird sinking feeling.

What?

The former CEO of Generation Healthcare, the family patriarch, the inestimable Gasper Cromwell is . . . Mr. Comstat?

I start to construct explanations for what I am seeing, but each one requires such a colossal twist of logic that my mind finally gives up. The *most* logical explanation, of course, is that the resemblance is merely that: a resemblance, the way each person has a doppelganger. I am able to rest comfortably in this thought until later in the day when, unable to help myself, I jump back on the computer for a little more research.

And learn that Gasper Cromwell went missing from Piedmont Hills Memory Care two years ago.

Piedmont Hills is a stunning facility. In the pictures, everyone is smiling and playing croquet. Even bingo looks like it could change your life. The website describes *luxury senior living* at an *appealing address* where, in addition to housekeeping, laundry, fitness gyms, and outdoor living spaces, members also enjoy personal chef–prepared meals. But apparently they sometimes lose people. Mr. Cromwell, it seems, was checked out by a daughter, a certain *Mimmy Cromwell*, who never returned him following an outing they went on two years ago. It took three weeks before anyone noticed he was gone.

From there, the trail runs cold. Articles mentioning his disappearance simply drop off, and the family is all smiles at a black-tie gala for Saint Francis Children's Hospital fully one year after their beloved Grandpa Cromwell went missing. The only subsequent reference discusses a lawsuit filed on behalf of the family seeking $10,000,000 in compensatory damages for *deficient security resulting in elder loss*.

And Mimmy Cromwell? There is no Mimmy Cromwell. But there is a nurse I know, a nurse named Mim, who is still, it would seem, on an outing with a certain patriarch of a billionaire family, an outing involving a *less appealing address*, an absence of chef-prepared meals, and a small outdoor patio with garden gnomes the only green space for miles.

Mim. What have you done?

There is a common saying in AA circles: keep your side of the street clean. This works, I guess, until someone has committed a crime on the other side of the street. But it is perhaps my current philosophy of "live and let live" (similar, of course, to the Live Free or Die motto of my adopted state) that keeps me from going directly to the police.

And there is also the unavoidable fact of, well, Mim being *good*. I mean, take the fan, which has blown away the blistering discomfort of my hot flashes for weeks now. It's more than that, though—strangely, *so much more*. In the course of any ordinary day—as we run our medications from room to room, delicately lifting a spoonful of non-poisoned soup to Lorna's mouth, clapping when Tom is finally picked up for his doctor's appointment (in a medical transport we pay for ourselves)—I have started to feel as though I am a part of something bigger than myself. In the heat of an argument about whether or not I am a communist, Don and I wave to George through his window, and *he waves back*. It's like this dilapidated old folks' home has turned into something beautiful, and Mim is kind of the beating heart at the middle of it all.

But it's something Mr. Comstat says that makes me realize I can't avoid the unavoidable, at least not forever. "I was snatched by those banjo dogs," he mutters, trying to push his wheelchair toward the door. "Those banjo dogs got me."

Three days later, Mim and I are laughing in the staff room—I was telling her how I once tried to go curb-jumping on my bicycle after an all-you-can-drink margarita lunch—and I happen to glance at her scrubs. I inadvertently gasp, then cough to cover it up. Her scrubs are covered in cartoon animals playing an assortment of musical instruments and—unmistakable, in the mix—there they are:

Dogs. Playing banjos.

I confront Mim the next day as she joins Mr. . . . Comstat and me on the patio. She arrives humming a Frank Sinatra tune, landing in an Adirondack chair with a deep sigh. I can't look at her and feel a rising hot flash as I blurt out, "Mim, I know who your 'father' really is," my fingers lifting into air quotes as I simultaneously cringe at how dumb that seems.

Mim stares at the ground for several seconds, then lifts her gaze to mine and sings the rest of her hummed song looking directly into my eyes. *I did it myyyyyy waaaay*. And then winks. "You are doing so much better than you realize. Told you that. Smart one. Saw it the minute I met you." Suddenly Mim's sweetness has an edge.

"I don't know what that means," I say, echoing the mantra of my current life.

"Darlin', the thing is, you *do* know. Maybe you've been medicating yourself into a state of denial for a few decades now, but you know."

"Where is my fucking accountant?" Mr. Comstat yells suddenly.

"He's on his way," Mim answers, placing a comforting hand on his shoulder. He settles immediately.

Through my new lens—the one where Mim has kidnapped Mr. Comstat—all her prior behavior takes on a different meaning. She has not been caring for him; she has been *tricking him*. Has she been doing the same to me? To all of us?

"I had no idea you were such a good liar," I say.

At this, Mim reaches for both of my hands. "We're all very good at lying," she says softly. Sadly. She tilts her head, but keeps her eyes sharply trained on my own.

"I don't lie," I say, jerking my hands away. "At least not now. And even when I drank, I wasn't lying to anyone but myself. And none of it was intentional. None of it was *planned*. None of it was *evil*."

"You think I'm evil?" Mim asks. She laughs a loud, slow laugh that lingers in the air once it's over. "Honey, I've seen evil, and it isn't me."

"I've seen some evil bullshit too," says Mr. Comstat. "Idiot sons. Never visit. Idiot wife." Mim pats him on the back, a move that previously would have seemed kind.

"Mim, you need to tell me. Just what exactly have you done?"

"You already know, just not the why of it. Give a guess," she says, with a wry smile.

"I think you kidnapped Gasper Cromwell and put him in here, where you have kept him for three years, tortured inside these dismal walls, stolen from his family who must be out of their minds with worry."

"That's correct. Well, except for the last part. The family isn't worried. They declared him dead a year ago, and it's actually streamlined the estate process to have him gone."

"I'm Gasper, who are you?" Mr. Comstat says.

"I'm your daughter Mimmie—you remember me, don't you?"

"Of course," Mr. Comstat says, a wide grin spreading across his face. "Of course I remember you! The kindest daughter I have ever known." His voice chokes and tears fill his eyes.

Mim turns back to me. "The only thing you need to ask yourself, in that quiet inner space only you can find, is what God's will looks like. God as you understand him. *Seeking only to do his will*—that's the eleventh, right? You get to be older like me and you start to see the world less like something that happens to you and more like something you participate in. Think of me like an agent of karma and mercy rolled into one—able to give a person a bitter glimpse of the world they built, with some sugar to make it go down a little easier. I'm just suggesting if someone spends their life building homes for old folks, shouldn't that be where they live, in the end?"

"How have you gotten away with this?" I whisper.

"Sweetheart, why don't you answer that question yourself."

The words have a slow cadence as they leave my mouth. "Because no one notices old people."

"No one notices," she echoes, her smile full of dark humor. "It's a freedom, really, but it can take a while to see it that way."

We've been out on the patio long enough now that the sun is starting to lower in the sky, sending long shadows that touch the plastic bird feeders and poorly trimmed bushes, the hard dirt where grass no longer grows, the ice patches that have yet to melt from the last rain-snow. A breeze blows through and my arms prickle, shoulders bracing against the cold.

"I want to go inside," Mr. Comstat says.

"Soon," Mim answers, not looking at him. Shadows are starting to furrow under her cheeks and nose. When she speaks, her voice is barely audible, low, deep. "See, my father died in a place just like this. I went to visit him on a Sunday morning and found him lying on the floor, pee and blood spilling from his body. The door was open, but nobody had seen him. No one knew how long he had been like that." She pauses and stares at the sky.

"I want to go inside," Mr. Comstat says.

"I'm so sorry," I say, shivering, which causes the words to stutter.

"Nah. It's not about condolences. It's not even about revenge, not anymore." Mim is still looking at the sky. It will be dark soon. We have been gone too long and have the evening medications to give out. "See, I used to be a lot like you, but that moment changed me. I decided to do something," Mim says. "You can't be afraid of doing something wrong—you won't do anything worse than Gasper over here. It's wrong to make the world eat where you shit. I guess I decided that's a meal we should at least share together."

"How many . . . others . . . are there?" I ask, my whole body shaking now, the shivering chopping up my words.

"Well, now, that, my dear, is between the good lord and me," Mim says, winking, her voice clear. "Think of this as a sanctuary. For difficult CEOs."

My contract ends on a Friday. Leaving Elm Garden feels like closing a too-full closet, where small, random objects keep falling into the door jamb; every time the door is shut, some tiny, red sleeve manages to peak through. Larry gives me a long hug and I let go too early. Dan gives me a copy of *The Conscience of a Conservative* by Barry Goldwater along with a nice card. Mim places her delicate hand on my chest, a little to the left, right where my heart is. We're nurses, after all—we know our anatomy.

"Mim?" I ask.

"What, darlin'?" she asks, but Lorna interrupts, scream-laughing as she grabs a completed puzzle and starts throwing pieces around the room. By the time I've calmed her down and gathered all the wayward bits of sky and little trees, Mim is gone.

I drive the few hours to Boston on automatic, darkness spreading along the crisscross of highways. As I near the city, I get the strangest feeling that I am somehow stationary, that it is the buildings that are moving closer, the world rushing toward me again, my old life and that now unfamiliar person I used to be. I am thinking. What looks like care can be a crime; what looks like a crime can be care. Sometimes it's all mixed up in the same thing. When do we call the cops? I don't know. But I know I won't call them on Mim.

As I pull onto my street, I abruptly realize that I'm no longer afraid I won't stay sober. Somewhere along the drive, my brain finished with that question—unconsciously, perhaps while I was sliding under the fiftieth overpass, that final neuron tipped over the edge and I just knew I wouldn't—run, escape, watch life pass as though I am not a part of it, hide because I am so afraid of it all. I just knew I wouldn't ever drink again.

Ode to Helene, October 2024

Barbara Roether

Now that you've gone
we see the shape of you everywhere.
The fallen trees all bowing in the empty direction of your exit
we marvel at the work you've left behind, warp and weft of
 your delicate hands weaving ten thousand leaves into the chain link fence,
wrapping the sign posts with plaited grass,
the darker takings we won't speak of
caress and flow
the humor with which you placed that open dishwasher so high in the tree,
 as if to curse all of domesticity forever.

You were a wild woman was why we loved you
loved your body when it rose from the bed
brown and brawny,
to fill the valley from edge to edge,
your joyous roar
psycho whore, Kali, Durga
our hearts longing to join in the dark force of your freedom.

Tarantulas in the Pumphouse

Linda Caradine

In June 1963, my family moved into a whitewashed clapboard house in rural Louisiana. It was much too small for a pair of adults and two kids, and I remember it had an awkward layout whereby one had to walk through the smaller bedroom to reach the kitchen. Presumably built by someone with no house-building experience or little common sense, it had to have been cheap and close to my dad's new army post at Fort Polk. As a six-year-old and a budding animal lover, I saw a new world of possibilities in and around that modest home. A wooded pine lot rose behind the house; a horse was in the corral across the gravel road, and a row of deserted doghouses were scattered beside the property. And there were very few people in this erstwhile neighborhood. At last, I was truly in my element.

Adventure loomed. I spent much time avoiding an overprotective mother and exploring my surroundings. A word about my mother: she embodied the term "helicopter parent" before it was conceived in modern parlance. She was smothering, domineering, intent on dousing whatever spark of wonder or imagination I held as a young girl. One might suppose she had a particularly jaundiced worldview owing to her own upbringing in Nazi Germany during the first half of the 20th century. Whatever the origin of her condition, she was a control freak.

But I digress. The woods loomed tall with an unlimited potential for impromptu wildlife spotting. With each cautious visit across the road, the neighbor's horse allowed me to approach closer and closer. And the doghouses stood silent sentry as so many would-be cabins for my newly tamed campground of squirrels, armadillos, and black snakes, species I had known previously only as roadkill. I had been taught to fear the world, but where real-world horrors plagued me—lessons well-learned from my mother—my six-year-old sense of newness took over.

I constructed a secret, magical organization around myself, a club I called Kreest, peopled with talking animals and friendly giants. Under their aegis, I was able to ignore the preached dangers of venomous creatures hiding under logs, a spooked half-ton horse waiting to trample me, and all manner of threats to my small and tender little life. But there was one chink in my armor, and every day before I ventured outside, I would be warned of it in no uncertain terms.

"Don't go near that pumphouse, Linda," my mom would shout out the back door after me. "There are tarantulas in there, and they bite."

"I won't," I would enthusiastically agree. Tarantulas were not among the animals that I loved. They were large and hairy with bulbous black eyes and death-dealing pincers. I avoided them at all costs. If I ventured too near, they would get me.

"And stay in the yard," she would holler, an all-around assurance that an expanse of short grass would protect me from the world writ large.

Of course, I ignored this final directive, heading immediately to the small woods behind the house. On one humid day, I found a box turtle; on another, I managed to trap a field mouse under a paper cup. I brought my new friends home and fashioned elaborate quarters for them in and around the shantytown of old doghouses. In time, I acquired a small dog and a pair of kittens, who joined me in ruling over my wild kingdom.

Kreest meetings were conducted down by the doghouses as well. These were joyous affairs, filled with clapping hands and the stomping of feet to accompany my raucous praise for the natural world. Perhaps, unknowingly, I had modeled Kreest after occasional visits to my grandfather's Baptist church services, which my brother and I were made to attend whenever we visited him. Kreest even sounded like Christ. But I was oblivious. The construct was mine and mine alone, and I believed in its tenets like a tiny Christian soldier.

I became acquainted with the lucky, slightly older girl across the way who owned the horse. She let me ride him once in a while, decked in his fancy western saddle and the bridle with silver rowels and leather embellishments swishing around my legs. I pretended I was a fearless knight prancing off to war instead of a timid little girl perched atop a fly-plagued nag. It was exhilarating. The world was mine.

But there was still the problem of the pumphouse, a bit of the empire that was off-limits to me and my magic. I worried about the tarantulas. Did they ever creep out of that dark, damp shed into the light of day? If so, it was possible they would get me. I had nightmares about pus-filled ulcers spreading up my chubby legs and the sickly reek of death hovering around me. I imagined losing my limbs to their poison. I envisioned the evil creatures getting tangled in my hair and hiding under my clothes, waiting to bite me. The tarantulas were my kryptonite, and I could not simply ignore them.

In my braver moments, I thought about stealing a can of Raid from under the kitchen sink and squirting it into the pumphouse before slamming the decrepit door and running away. I considered setting it on fire with my mother's matches. I wanted to use my brother's chemistry set to blow it to smithereens. I hoped for a Louisiana tornado or monsoon rain to wash them into another parish. Mostly, I expected (dare I say prayed?) the sublime power of Kreest to protect me.

One morning, I woke before everyone else and ventured outside, still in my PJs, to feed lettuce to my growing stable of turtles. The sun was partially out, and a delicate lace of dew danced atop the lawn before my every tentative step. As I sat cross-legged atop one of the old doghouses, tossing big leaves of greenery into the turtle pen below, I sensed a barely perceptible scrabbling off to my left side. Looking down, I saw one of the dreaded tarantulas taking some fresh air on the lawn before the day's heat set in. It was even more horrifying than I had imagined, with a midnight-black body, evil swiveling eyes, and nervous, twitching legs covered in stubbly hairs— the better to pinpoint my location with. I was frozen with fear.

After a moment, I regained my sensibilities enough to chuck the plastic lettuce bowl at the wretched thing, hoping to frighten it back into the pump house from whence it came. It scurried away, leaving a higgledy-piggledy trail in the morning dew and breaking the spell.

After that, I was careful not to venture out too early. Instead, I would spend my morning hours preening in the bathroom and dawdling over my breakfast. I didn't want to risk meeting up with another of the tarantulas anytime soon. This wasn't the first time my mom's dire warnings had rung true. She had a way of knowing about dangerous things and things to be avoided at all costs. She referred to them as *verboten* and repeatedly ensured I got the message loud and clear.

Over time, I found myself wondering whether it was these evil, dangerous entities or her harsh admonishments themselves that were more frightening. As a precocious child, it didn't escape me that the tarantula hadn't hurt me. It was her scorching words of warning that had wounded my soul and frightened me into playing indoors on most subsequent mornings.

And, of course, it wasn't only the tarantulas.

According to my mother, the world was chockful of dangers. Everything from skulking child killers to poisoned apples, from a misstep off a slippery path to an encounter with a mad dog, could kill me. I didn't know if everyone knew of these dangers and feared them or if I was particularly weak and susceptible in my mother's eyes. My naïve child's mind had me believing the latter. Thus, in trying to keep me safe, my mother had taken away my power.

Ill-prepared as I was to navigate the world, my penchant for make-believe filled the spaces left in my character. I invented Kreest. I dwelt in my little magical realm, where guiding fairies and protective beasts allowed me to move about my enchanted landscape. This fairy dust approach worked sufficiently well until I started school. School was its own unique horror show and existed devoid of all supernatural sources of safety and confidence. For some reason, Kreest, and thus my protective imaginary life, didn't exist once I boarded the bus each morning.

I could operate boldly only when I was home, alone, and I took every advantage of that detail. When no one was around, I was Wonder Woman, He-Man, and the Incredible Hulk all rolled into one. I would be indestructible if I could just find a way to banish those tarantulas. It occurred then that perhaps those dreadful spiders were my mother's creation, brought into being as a mechanism for keeping me pliant and needful. And how could I ever hope to battle that?

So, I spent as much time as possible in the shady, cut-short backyard, where anything seemed possible. I hunted for critters that might venture out of the woods and near the house and added old boards to my maze of pens and fences daily. I celebrated Kreest. I picnicked on sandwiches and corn chips under the gnarly pecan tree that stood sentry out back. And I went into the house each night feeling fairly pleased by my day's exploits.

The time came when, inevitably, my mother announced that it was time to move again to accommodate my dad's most recent military service assignment. It was the end of everything. I could only acknowledge the news without protest and go about the sad duty of releasing my turtles and other animals, tearing down the pens, and saying goodbye to the horse and his owner. No one thought to ask a quiet little girl her opinion. No one considered what would be best for her. Moving was an adult matter. All I could do was go along.

This time, we ended up in Springfield, Missouri's nondescript Bible Belt enclave. There were no woods, no animals, and no magic. Kreest had faded into the background and was replaced by fourth-grade hell at yet another new school. But I continued to survive. I grew, and in time, I became a young woman with much angst and many untended dreams. I knew how to care for myself and move relatively smoothly through life from one milestone to the next. But, inside, I was still grappling with the unfinished childhood business of weighing whether I was loved and valued, needing very much to feel a sense of personal agency, and having to say goodbye again and again. I never got past the vague feeling that I was just some inanimate object being moved from place to place on a giant gameboard. I never recovered from all that early loss.

As an adult, the source of my trauma had evolved into a nameless mass at the base of my brain, ready to spring into being like a tarantula from his lair anytime life became new or challenging or in any way provocative. It was in this tormented state that I managed to move from one place and one career and one relationship to another. It was only after several years of this existential struggle that the edges of the mass began to wear away and grow smooth.

Eventually, encroaching old age brought with it the relative freedom born of life experience. I had come to know that certain things could not hurt me. Oh, the tarantulas were still there, but they seemed to stay out of sight in the pumphouse on most days. I could finally be carefree for all I had missed along the way. I could trek into the deep woods of my imagination and come out unscathed.

I learned to enjoy the wisdom, experience, and perspective only time can provide. I have developed a clearer sense of judgment, focusing on what truly matters. Stronger emotional resilience helps me handle life's challenges with a note of grace. And deeper relationships with family and friends bring greater fulfillment. All told, I've found increased happiness and contentment, appreciating life's simple joys. In moments of introspection, I wonder if any of this richness would have been possible had I not glimpsed the tarantulas lurking there in that obscure Louisiana pumphouse. I wonder if it was Kreest that saved me.

For the Birds

Emily France

Red-shouldered hawk perched on a power pole
Tawny feathers fluffed
Her head pivots back and forth
Raptor eyes scanning the stretch of snowy grass below

I wonder if she knows how lovely she is
The noble outline of her body
The lethal hook of her beak
The promise of her folded wings
That compel you to picture them soaring
Power without apology
She takes without asking

Once, I too was beautiful and untethered
Commanding attention with the blinding neon of youth alone
I didn't realize it then but
I was deadly in my taking
Striking from an imposing height
And leaving only scraps for the scavengers
Still I hungered for more

These days I am more like the house finch at my feeder
Flustered and fidgeting
Feathers a steely brown to better blend in
She still feeds her full-grown babies from last spring
They line up on the deck rail waiting
Chirping and impatient
For her to deposit seed into their mouths

Once admired from below
A flash of burnished orange in the treetops
Now foraging, fading into the underbrush
Flitting from feeder to fledgling
The quiet work of keeping something alive

The finch goes still, listening
Then launches into the air with a quickness that stuns
Wings spreading wide
Her flight is smaller, less lofty
But it still looks like soaring to me

Moose

Nancy L. Davis

after Elizabeth Bishop

Summer of '65, family road trip to Maine,
simple memories haunt: prying loose white
lobster flesh, rocky coastlines, slippery granite
slabs, Acadia National Park in the local news

as we left home: a boy of ten lost in northern
woods. We knew the family, members of our church,
saw them Sundays in congregational pews.

Years later, my own family in Maine, my daughter
roughly the same age I'd been, we hiked Acadia,
a coastline trail—not deep into the unforgiving forest.

Stone cairn markers, some toppled and missing,
misguided us. The sun dipped; ocean breezes lashed
in late summer chill. We shivered in khakis and cotton.
Don't tell her we're lost.

Danny, the boy, never was found.

Lichen-covered rock exposed layers
of life, of death. Village lights clustered
below, exiling us to a cruel tangle of nowhere.

How to cope?

My daughter saw it first: bull moose, statuesque, musk
driven and silent, steam rising from the push and heave
of majestic bearing. It turned its massive head toward us,
butterflied antlers years in the making.

This beast, at home, not lost.

Snorting, it ambled across and down the behemoth rock
with improbable grace, disappearing into the violet void of
dusk. With flashlight pointed forth, I found one cairn
and another, a third, a fourth. Trembling, we traversed

the rocks, this way and that, in rip-rap rhythm, cautious
and alert, thoughts blending in chowder and warmth.

In bed, safe and found, I marveled at fortune, asked,
Who'd sent this talisman? Advanced in age and scope,
Who had held out hope?

In Another Life—a Dream Tied to a Mesquite Tree

Mary Ann Burrows

In another life, I lived in an apartment—cinder block walls painted beige, a balcony too small to sit on, its rusted railing wobbling when you leaned, overlooking a parking lot cracked with weeds and oil stains, where stray cats prowled, and air conditioners droned on.

The smell of someone else's dinner clung to the plaster—burnt onions, cheap takeout, burnt popcorn—seeping into the carpet, matted gray, worn down by years of pacing. The ceiling fan wobbled, its pull chain a small shell my mom brought back from Hawaii, its weathered blades spinning in an uneven rhythm. Light from a flickering neon sign outside sneaked in through the blinds, and the nights were heavy with the sound of faraway trains, car alarms, and the muffled voices of neighbors arguing, laughing, having wild sex with strangers. A place that rattled alive in its own quiet, decaying way.

I stood there on that tiny balcony, leaning against the railing, staring out at nothing, pretending the world couldn't see me, aching for something more.

Sometimes, I drank instant coffee straight from the jar, black powder dissolving on my tongue. Other times, I mixed it with boiled water, added mushroom powder I bought off Amazon, and sugar packets stolen from the diner on 8th Street—those little ones with sticky edges that smelled faintly of syrup.

No bees, no honey, no hives humming. No chickens running in the backyard like I once dreamed. Just Harold, my half-bald mutt, and a fridge with a buzz—so loud I slept with the door closed at night, or talked to my friends on the phone in my bedroom because I couldn't hear my own voice.

The neighbors screamed most nights, slamming doors so hard the walls shook. I didn't know their names, but I imagined them—the guy in 3C who chain-smoked on the fire escape, waiting

for a job that never came. The woman beside me who blasted old country songs and laughed and knocked her bed frame against the wall, waking me up every night at exactly 3 a.m.

We lived alone, together—our lives pressed up against each other like bad wallpaper.

The nights smelled like asphalt, liquor sweating through cracks. I walked my dog under streetlights that buzzed like dying flies, holding my keys tight in my palm, sticking one out between my pointer and middle fingers—just in case somebody jumped me outside the convenience store or laundromat. I counted the steps between nowhere and nowhere else.

One day, the longing became too much. Maybe it was something small that broke—another ceiling leak from the toilet upstairs, the fridge finally giving out, or Harold getting sick again all over my dirty carpets. And then I realized: if I stayed there, I might never leave. I would die in that apartment. They would find me and my faithful companion weeks later, on the floor, both stiff, the TV still on, the fan clicking, the shell pull-chain my mom gave me still swinging, the air thick with it—the slow rot of something left too long a sickly sweetness under the stench of unwashed dishes. Days would pass before anyone noticed.

I came across an Airstream trailer, corroding in the corner of some old scrapyard. I patched the holes with duct tape, sold everything I owned for gas money, loaded Harold into the passenger seat of a friend's truck I borrowed, and headed south.

Along the way, I joined a women's liberation group, started smoking Virginia Slims because they gave them away for free at meetings. It became a habit I never kicked, just another weight I carried—thin and burning, like the pull in my chest.

I unofficially changed my name to Sky, renamed my dog Bo, and took that Airstream trailer, eventually crossing the border, then a ferry to the Baja Peninsula—the kind of place where the air smelled like salt and dirt, where the stars looked like spilled salt against the black.

I ended up in Todos Santos, parked the trailer ten miles out by the ocean on Los Cerritos Beach, hung my laundry between two trees, grew my now-white hair long, wore a flower crown, sang

around the fire and handwrote poems in calligraphy using a found Varsity fountain pen on strips of torn recycled paper bags.

I hung these poems on thrift-store ribbons like art, tying them to the branches of a Mesquite tree on the corner of La Esquina (Calle Topete & Horizonte), where tourists and wanderers stopped for coffee and conversation. The twisted limbs of the Mesquite cradled my words, waiting for the right hands. People found them—read them, then somehow found me by the ocean—sometimes leaving a loaf of bread, a bag of blood oranges, or dog food for Bo in return, like we had some unspoken deal: their kindness for my small, quiet offerings.

Maybe the emptiness stayed, settling in like an unwanted roommate. But maybe, just maybe, it felt lighter there. The air smelled different. The sounds were different—children laughing, waves lapping against the shore, fires crackling, voices carrying in the dusk.

The salty breeze carried the green tang of leaves mixed with Virginia Slims, the warmth of sunbaked wood, the smoke of fires curling into the night. And something else—something unnameable, lighter than emptiness, the pause that hung between the branches, in the words I left for strangers.

I was happy there by the fire, writing under the stars, the tide lapping against the shore, the earth beneath me, roots shifting in the dark knowing my voice swayed in the breeze from a Mesquite tree nearby. And if I died there, someone might notice, find me with my dog curled up on my lap and a smile on my face.

And for once, I didn't ache for anything more.

Contributors

ALLYSON PETREK is an emerging fiction writer based in Cincinnati, Ohio. Her debut short story was recently named the first-place winner in the adult prose category of the 2024 Books by the Banks festival. As a wife and a mother of two young children, she is inspired by the adventures of motherhood and all of the strong, wild women in her life.

ALEXIS BONAVITACOLA, PHD, is a writer, artist, and lifelong educator based in Philadelphia. She earned her PhD at 59 and, in her 50s, discovered painting—eventually building an international art community and teaching thousands of students to embrace their artistic selves. She considers herself a steward of her students' dreams, always empowering women—especially those in midlife and beyond—to see their potential and confidently walk through doors of possibility. Now, at 70, she embraces the next creative chapter as an emerging writer and believes it's never too late to begin again. "Cedar Woman," her first published essay, explores transformation through heartbreak, humor, resilience, and spiritual awakening. She credits her husband, John—a brilliant writer—with inspiring her to take risks on the page and honor her own voice. When she's not writing or painting, you'll find her reading voraciously or relishing treasured moments with her family. Her next project will honor her late brother's legacy through a visual memoir-in-fragments—a creative blend of art, text, and memory, illuminating his life one image, one word, one story at a time.

IZZY FORREST-SMITH lives in a small mountain town in Colorado and currently works in LGBTQ+ healthcare via telehealth. Most of their poems are inspired by nature and living in a rural town as a queer person. When they are not writing, they are most likely running on the trails with friends, taking their dogs to the river with their spouse, or reading a really good book.

HAYA POMRENZE's poems have appeared in numerous journals, including *Hanging Loose*, *Rattle*, *Hawaii Pacific Review*, *Paterson Literary Review*, *Lake Effect*, and *MiPOesis*. She is the author of two poetry collections, *Hook* (Rock Press, 2007), a National Jewish Book Award nominee, and *How It's Done* (Finishing Line Press, 2014). Haya is an occupational therapist who uses poetry as a healing tool on a psychiatric unit. She considers herself the founder of the Jewhitsu poetry form. An award-winning storyteller, Haya has a second career as a spoken word performer.

MARSH ROSE is a psychotherapist and freelance writer living in northern California. Her essays and short stories have appeared in a variety of publications including *Cosmopolitan* magazine, *Salon.com*, the *San Francisco Chronicle*, *Hippocampus* magazine, and others. Her essay, "False Memory," won first prize for creative nonfiction from New Millennium Writing in 2018. Marsh's memoir, *A Version of the Truth*, is in press with Sunbury Press.

JENNA A. SMITH is a Texas-based writer interested in promoting the inner strength of women facing adversity. Writing about the power of the Feminine She in Nature is her passion. She is entering the MFA Program for Writers at Warren Wilson College this summer and will concentrate in poetry. "Feed her" is her first published poem, which she happily dedicates to that "rusty red horse" from her childhood, burrs and all. She currently lives in Austin with her spouse and four children.

BARRY FIELDS lives with his wife and dog in the mountains of North Carolina. His recent short stories have been published or are soon to be published in *Sundial: A Magazine of Literary Historical Fiction*, *New English Review*, *Ginosko Literary Journal*, the *Pennsylvania Literary Journal*, *After Dinner Conversation*, Storm Dragon Publishing, *The Rumen*, and others. Two of his earlier short stories placed in contests, and numerous nonfiction articles have appeared in a variety of publications.

JENNIFER SCHOLLARS works as a mental health therapist and uses nonfiction storytelling to explore personal themes of authenticity, identity, and belonging. She resides in Missouri with her two cats and ever-growing indoor garden.

NOEL PLENNERT POSTON is an inquisitive seeker who writes poetry because nothing else lasts like a good poem. She has been enamored of words and especially poetry ever since she can remember. And she hopes to write in a way that challenges and encourages others to seek their own way through words. Nothing is as satisfying as crafting a poem that gets it right, tells it just the way you want to tell it. And nothing is finer than reading a well-crafted poem.

SHAKIRA CROCE is a poet living in Lynbrook, New York. Her poetry chapbook, *Leave It Raw* (Finishing Line Press, 2020), has received critical acclaim by New Books Network, California State Poetry Society, Mom Egg Review, and others. Her poetry has been published widely in literary magazines and journals, including the *Cordite Poetry Review*, *New Ohio Review*, *Permafrost* magazine, Pilgrimage Press, *Sequestrum*, and *Vassar Review*. She graduated with a BA from Sarah Lawrence College and an MPA from Pace University. Shakira currently works as director of communications and public relations at Amida Care, New York's largest special needs health plan, supporting underserved populations living with HIV and trans individuals.

AYLA GARD is an Australian environmental writer based in Los Angeles. Across fiction, nonfiction, and poetry, her work explores biodiversity loss, urban ecology, and the often-complicated relationships between people and nature. She is completing an MFA in Nature Writing at Western Colorado University, and her work has appeared elsewhere in *Orion* and *Scientific American*. You can find her on Instagram @aylagardening.

CARLA VIANNA is a Brazilian-American writer, photographer, and lifelong traveler currently rooted in Rio de Janeiro. A journalist by trade, she began her career in traditional newsrooms in Miami and New York City before pivoting to creative writing, drawing from her global travels and personal experiences with love, loss, identity, and healing. Her poetry explores the liminal space between heartbreak and healing, identity and belonging, home and the open road. Her work is an invitation—to return to ourselves, to question everything, and to find beauty in both the breaking and the becoming. Carla's journalism work has appeared in *Eater, Condé Nast Traveler*, and the *Washington Post*. She is currently working on her debut poetry collection. Find her writing and photography on Instagram @bycarlavianna and on her travel blog, travelbycarlavianna.com.

COURTNEY HANKS is a writer and illustrator based in Central Florida. She holds a BFA in creative writing from the University of Central Florida and is currently pursuing an MFA in prose at Stetson University. She is drawn to narratives that explore beauty, wonder, and human vulnerability.

ERIN DiCAMILLO is an emerging poet who rediscovered her love of the craft while navigating early motherhood, a cross-country move, a pandemic, wildfires, and several reconstructive hip surgeries. Poetry became her recipe for a beautiful, complex life with all its ingredients and cross currents. She graduated from the University of Michigan with degrees in English and Spanish, and worked in political campaigns, charter schools, and tech companies. She now focuses her time on her family and teaching Pilates. She lives in Louisville, Colorado, with her husband and son. When she's not in presence with her family or writing, you can find her hunting down or preparing delicious food and exploring the world through movement of every kind.

JULIA BURKE is a Jersey girl and author of the poetry book *Moonstruck: Told by the Seasons*. She also has a new collection in the works, capturing the beauty and chaos of being a twentysomething. When she's not penning poems—or gathering the experiences that inspire them (catching flights, getting lost in her latest read, etc.)—Julia continues to master her craft as a copywriter at an advertising agency. Follow her writing journey on Instagram: @j_burke_poetry and @juliaburke816.

ANNEKE BENDER is a writer, teacher, and physical therapist living in Atlanta, GA. Her short stories, poems, and essays explore themes of loss, magical wandering, and the inner landscape of the body. Her work has previously appeared in *Fish Anthology 2023* from Fish Publishing. When not working, she can be found napping for pleasure, strolling the historic cemetery near her home, and riding her bike in strange lands.

LINDA CARADINE is an award-winning Oregon writer. Her work has appeared in a variety of literary journals, magazines, newspapers, and online. Her 2024 memoir, titled *Lying Down with Dogs*, was published by Unsolicited Press in Portland, OR. In addition to writing, Linda started and runs a nonprofit animal rescue organization.

EMILY FRANCE is a writer and communications professional based in Ypsilanti, Michigan. Her work explores themes of inheritance, identity, and transformation, often through the lens of motherhood, mental health, and place. While a longtime writer, she is relatively new to publishing and thrilled to have her work recognized in TulipTree Publishing's Wild Women contest. When not writing or working, she enjoys knitting, exploring the outdoors with her rescue dogs, and being mom to a delightfully neurodivergent three-year-old. This is one of her first publications, and she is grateful to be in the company of other wild women and those who write about them.

NANCY L. DAVIS has poems in *Cutthroat, Best of Philadelphia Stories, The Dewdrop*, the *Banyan Review, SuperPresent, Amethyst Journal, Evening Street Review, Connecticut River Review* (forthcoming), *The Orchards Poetry Journal*, and others. Her work has been awarded a Pushcart Prize nomination, first place in the Sandy Crimmins National Poetry Prize, second place in the Chicagoland Patrons & Poets' 67th Poetry Award, finalist in the Joy Harjo Poetry Prize, and the *Atlanta Review* International Merit Award. *Ghosts*, her chapbook, was published in 2019 by Finishing Line Press. In 2020, her poems were long-listed for the Disquiet Literary Seminar in Lisbon, and again in 2022 for the Bedford International Prize in Poetry. She lives and writes in Park Ridge, IL, and Long Beach, IN, on Lake Michigan, after a long career as associate professor of English at Harper College in Illinois.

MARY ANN BURROWS is a Canadian writer, poet, and artist whose work gently explores the intersections of nature, resilience, and the untamed human spirit. Her writing is rooted in a deep connection to the land and a lifelong commitment to creative expression as a means of healing and transformation. She is the author of *The Last Hurrah: A Living Workbook for a Happy Ending*, a guided legacy and end-of-life planning book inspired by her experience as a certified death doula. She has also written two illustrated children's books focused on emotional well-being and self-awareness: *Oh, Monkey!* and *Gator on My Back*. Her essays and poetry have appeared in several creative and therapeutic writing anthologies, including *The Creativity Workbook for Coaches and Creatives* (Routledge, 2021), *Transformational Journaling for Coaches, Therapists, and Clients* (Routledge, 2021), and *The Great Book of Journaling* (Mango Media, 2022). Mary Ann lives on a 72-acre farm outside Vancouver, where she grows wildflowers for bees, walks the forest trails, and tends to the quiet rhythms of the natural world. Her work is a reflection of this landscape—tender, grounded, and alive with meaning.

www.ingramcontent.com/pod-product-compliance
Lightning Source LLC
Chambersburg PA
CBHW082047220626
47052CB00007B/1244